Alice,

From one aspiring writer to another I wish you luck! I hope you enjoy your book.

Billy

TIMENOT

by

Billy G. Sandlin

FOREWORD

The setting for *TimeNot* is Eastern North Carolina from the 1940's through the 1970's. Some accounts are accurate. Some are imagined. Some names were changed to protect the innocent. Some names were changed to protect the guilty. Some names were changed to protect the author. The story is fiction. But even when changes were made, the resulting scenarios remained vintage Eastern North Carolina.

The feelings examined are real and vintage Anywhere, Planet Earth.

International Standard Book Number
ISBN 0-9661336-0-9

Printed in the United States of America

PURCHASING INFORMATION: The purchase price of this book is $16.00 plus a sales tax of $.96 (if purchased in North Carolina) and a shipping-and-handling charge of $4.00 if purchased by mail. If not found in book stores or on the Internet, it may be purchased by mailing the purchase price, plus fees as set forth above, by check or money order to the author at his law office at 220 New Bridge St., Jacksonville, NC 28540.

CONTENTS

Continued on next page.

SAFE HARBOR

An urgent call, join the race.
An initial stumble from starting gate,
Managed so well by youthful grace,
Though running sideways at its pace.

Delightful passions beckon ahead,
No tagging along, participate!
A call to the wild, don't hesitate,
With bended mind, judgment abates.

Necessities of life, a softer nest,
That house of cards teetering in winds,
A deceptive leader dragging all,
Kicking and screaming in its wake.

The masterful drummer, time dictates,
A trip with nary a stopping place.
Compelled to go, don't spectate,
Temporal things the object of gait.

Cast aside, anchors away,
Sail your ship with helm in hand,
None but thee heave to and fro,
Safe harbor is inward not yonder towed.

A resting place,
For the careful and quiet,
Sheltered from time,
In this search for life.

Eternity's gateway,
Though entered by night,
A walk with God,
A union with Light.

WHAT PROBLEM?

"I'm beginning to worry about our baby," Bess said to her husband, Alf.

"What's the matter?" he questioned.

"Well, Andy's a year old and he doesn't talk. His 'daddy' and 'mommy' are very few, and you have to keep after him to repeat those words. He doesn't even seem to want to talk. If you hand him an object, he hesitates to take it. He just looks. You have to force him. He seems interested enough, but he just looks. And have you noticed? He never cries."

"That's a blessing," Alf interrupted.

Bess continued. "I've given him little pinches and he just frowns. He has to be in some real pain before he cries, and then he doesn't cry for long. He hasn't even cried while teething. He just seems awfully passive."

"Doesn't sound like much to me," Alf said, "but if you want to, we can have the doctor check him out."

Bess made an appointment and had Andy examined.

"I cannot detect anything organically wrong," said the doctor. "He may just be a little slow."

"Do you mean retarded, stupid, or anything like that?" Bess was scared.

"No, no, nothing like that. We'll just have to wait a little longer and see how he develops. I wouldn't worry just yet. He has plenty of growing to do."

Bess kept a close eye on Andy. At two years old, Andy still had said little more than 'mommy' and 'daddy' when his vocabulary began to grow at a faster pace. Bess relaxed somewhat. But his responses to conversation were delayed. Talking with Andy took patience. He played with his toys in the same manner. Toys were to be observed before use.

Bess finally concluded to Alf in a motherly, protective, even defensive, manner. "Andy is intelligent enough. His delayed responses, and I prefer to say calculated responses, do give me cause for concern. But I think he is so satisfied just to observe that it hardly occurs to him that it's his turn. He is content to watch things happen. And trying to hurry Andy just results in more delays while he examines any attempt to hurry him." Bess paused. "I prefer to say that he has his own pace."

Alf came to appreciate Andy's 'pace'. He took the five-year-old fishing. He explained that the fish were in the water and threw the hook, worm, and line into the water. He explained further that the cork would move under the water when a fish would bite the worm. Andy listened. He was mesmerized. He sat staring at the cork for forty-five minutes until it finally moved.

"Pull on the pole, Andy."

Andy sat looking.

Alf pulled in the fish. "Now be ready to pull next time."

erfectly still with the pole in his hand until the next bite. :ork went under, and after his usual delay and ient from Alf, he pulled. He had caught his first fish.

ıf Alf sat Andy under a tree and told him to wait while he filled his dump truck with dirt, Andy waited - for the three hours of loading. If Alf said he would be home by 6:00, Andy had no trouble waiting by the door until 8:00. If Alf said wait while he talked business with a trucking partner, Andy waited.

"I do believe you'd sit there through an earthquake," Alf said to Andy after one particularly long wait.

This 'pace' would define Andy. He was patient to his mother. He was enduring to his father. He was retarded to some unkind classmates in grade school. However, by the time he reached high school, had learned to cope with his pace, and had earned good grades, he was cogitative.

Time would best define Andy's pace.

THE BEAST

A beast in the jungle,
The warning sound blared;
Stand clear of his presence,
To stop is to stare.

I sprang to my feet,
Chancing a glance;
His beauty was awesome,
As I stood transfixed.

'Here, killy', I beckoned,
Not knowing his breed,
But he clawed my hand,
Leaving me to bleed.

Refusing to look,
I turned my head,
But the vision remained,
Indelibly etched.

I ran from his presence,
Fleeing the beast,
But foreseeing each path,
He waited to feast.

Desperate for rest,
I retreated once more;
I hoped to safety,
And healing for sores.

But discerning my sanctuary,
He burst inside,
My secret place vulnerable,
Unable to hide.

Bound by folly,
He couldn't snare me,
But neither could I escape;
A tether bound me.

THE GIRL NEXT DOOR

The girl next door didn't live just next door. She lived in Greenville, which is sixty miles north and east of Richlands. Richlands is three miles from Haw Branch. Haw Branch was where Andy lived. Her name was Emily. Emily was shy. She was tender-hearted. She would cry at sad movies.

"Aunt Janie is here, Emily. Come and say hello," said Katie to the five-year-old Emily. Katie is Emily's mother.

Emily ran and peered from behind the nearest chair at Aunt Janie.

"Don't be shy," said Aunt Janie, Katie's sister.

Emily moved further behind the chair. Her peering was now a peeping.

"My, I can see you have grown a lot since I last saw you."

Emily disappeared completely behind the chair.

"Now, sweetheart. You remember Aunt Janie," said Katie.

"We'll give her some time, Katie," Janie said as she took her seat on the couch. "I could sure use something to drink. That trip from Raleigh leaves a body thirsty."

"I'll be right back," Katie said as she left for the kitchen. "Emily, come help mommy pour some tea."

Emily reluctantly followed her mother into the kitchen.

"Now, Emily, Aunt Janie has come a long way to see us so you be nice to her. She's my sister and she's not going to hurt you. She has no little girl of her own so she will probably want to be your friend. Do you think you can help me serve her some tea?"

"Yes, ma'am."

"Well, carry this glass to her then."

Emily eased up close to Aunt Janie and offered the tea without a word.

"My, aren't we helpful? Thank you."

"You're welcome," said Emily as she retreated to her mother's side. She then watched as Katie and Janie talked most of the afternoon away about this and that. They sipped their tea. Emily finally relaxed enough to take a seat halfway between Aunt Janie and Katie. She felt her face turn red when the conversation turned to her.

"Katie tells me you are learning to play the piano, Emily. Is that true?"

"Yes ma'am."

"Do you think you could play something for me?"

Emily looked at her mother.

"Go ahead. Aunt Janie would like to hear you play."

Emily went to the piano and played three scales and *Mary Had A Little Lamb*. She then again retreated to her mother's side.

"Very good. Not one mistake that I could detect," said Aunt Janie.

Before the weekend visit was over, Emily warmed to Aunt Janie. She sat next to Aunt Janie on the couch and allowed Aunt Janie to place her arm around her as they read a book together. Aunt Janie also got to hug Emily after they had played the piano together.

"Since we have become friends, Emily, do you think you might like to spend a weekend in Raleigh with me? Your mother can come too. And you could stop at the state park in Goldsboro and see all the flowers. They are pretty this time of year."

"Yes, ma'am."

"We'll have to get your mother to do that just as soon as we can."

Emily did spend weekends with Aunt Janie. She also stopped by the state park in Goldsboro which was especially beautiful in the springtime. When she was older, she would sojourn there at least once each spring just to enjoy the flowers.

GRADE SCHOOL

The school house was the biggest building Andy had ever seen. It was also the scariest. The halls stretched on forever. What in the world could be down there? The rooms were cavernous. Plenty of room for a little fellow to get lost. Andy held tightly to his mother's hand as she led him to the registration desk. What kind of place was this going to be when you had to take shots with big long needles just to get in? This would not be fun.

Andy endured as he usually did. Not one word did he utter. He just followed instructions.

"Place your head on your desk, students. It is time for a nap." Andy did.

"Get in line, students. We are going to lunch." Andy did.

"Get your coloring books out, children." Andy did.

"Stay in your seats while I'm out of the room." Andy did.

The school year was into its third week before Mrs. Garnto, Andy's first grade teacher, realized that she had not heard Andy say a single word. He had not even talked with the other children.

"What is your name?" She finally decided to get Andy to speak.

Andy just bowed his head and looked at his feet.

"Is your name Andy?"

y finally shook his head.

"Well, Andy, how are you liking school?"

Andy smiled.

"You can talk to me, Andy. I'm here to help you learn."

Andy kept smiling.

"Do you know my name?"

Andy shook his head indicating a yes.

"What is my name?"

Andy labored to respond and finally said, "Mrs. Garnto."

"That's right," Mrs. Garnto said encouragingly. Satisfied that he could at least talk, she finally said, "Well, I can see that you are going to be a quiet little boy. You may take your seat now. If you have anything to say, just raise your hand to let me know. I'll listen to you."

Andy nodded a yes as he took his seat. But he did not raise his hand the whole year.

A talk with Andy's mother at the first parent/teacher meeting helped Mrs. Garnto understand.

"Andy's not a slow learner, Mrs. Garnto; he's just slow to respond. He grasps most problems quickly enough. He just hesitates to act on his understanding of the problem," Bess said, displaying her protective, motherly instincts.

Mrs. Garnto expressed her concerns. "I was afraid we might have to place him in a class for special-needs children. Whenever I ask him to count, there is his usual delay. The other children laugh, which distracts him. He simply hesitates for a longer period. More laughter and so on. I have tried to get the children to be patient, but children can be cruel without knowing it."

"That sounds like Andy," Bess said.

"I must say the little fellow endures the laughter without apparent harm. If it bothers him I cannot detect it. Some children cry if laughed at. Not Andy. It's just another situation to be observed for him."

"Sounds just like Andy," Bess repeated.

With much patience and a lot of coaxing, Mrs. Garnto helped Andy complete the first grade.

The second grade was more of the same, with Andy learning to be more responsive. Written tests were a new experience, however. When Mrs. Parker, his second grade teacher, collected the first spelling test, Andy's paper was blank.

She asked Andy to stay behind after school. "Andy, didn't you know how to spell any of today's words?"

"Yes ma'am. I forgot to write them down, Mrs. Parker."

"Spell 'swim' for me."

"S-W-I-M."

"That's right. Now spell 'water'."

"W-A-T-E-R."

Andy could spell all l5 words on the test correctly.

"Why didn't you write the answers on your paper, Andy?"

"I don't know exactly, Mrs. Parker. When you said 'water', I started thinking about boats and fish and digging worms."

"Next time please remember to write your answers if it's a written test."

"Yes, ma'am."

Andy had learned once again that he was not a spectator but a participant. Andy would reach high school before he learned to manage his hesitancy and improve his grades. It would also be high school before classmates stopped laughing. There they came to expect a thoughtful and correct answer.

But Andy's pace continued to define him.

GRANDPARENTS
(Values Passed Down)

Andy spent much of the summers with his grandparents. They were 'Grandpa' and 'Grandma' to Andy. They were farmers and had always been. Grandpa was a burly man, six feet tall, 235 pounds, and strong. He could carry a two-hundred pound bag of fertilizer under each arm. He could load a lightwood stump into a trailer by himself. He could lift the corner of a stuck automobile from the mud. He could wrestle a sick cow to the ground and hold her there for treatment. To Andy he was a giant of a man.

And grandpa had time for children. At the beginning of each summer he would announce, "I think it's time for a new diving board for the swimming hole." A trip to the sawmill would follow.

Andy stood by grandpa before a big pile of logs. "Which log do you think would make the best diving board, Andy?" grandpa asked.

Andy stared at the big pile. Grandpa's question had made him feel important. He began to search for the right log.

"How about this one?" grandpa suggested.

"Yes, sir. I think that one will do just fine," Andy said proudly.

Andy watched as a big cable was hooked to the log and it was pulled into the sawmill.

"Make it twelve feet long, eighteen inches wide, and five inches thick," grandpa instructed.

Andy watched as the big six-foot saw blade began to slowly turn and then increase speed until its sound was a steady hum. It bit into the log with a shrill. A board cut to grandpa's specifications finally emerged on the conveyor belt.

"Did you see how that was done, Andy?" grandpa asked.

Andy nodded.

Grandpa was always teaching. "This is how to do this," he would say to any child who would listen. And in Andy he found a dedicated listener. Grandpa would teach; Andy would listen. Andy learned how to hook a mule to a cart, chop wood, stoke the wood-heated barn, crop tobacco, cure tobacco, milk a cow, and gather eggs. And he learned to work.

Another lesson concerned money. Grandpa had a saying, "A hundred days, a hundred dollars." Andy figured it came from grandpa's younger days when that actually was the wage for a day's work. When it came time to pay farm help for putting in the tobacco crop, grandpa would always holler, "A hundred days, a hundred dollars." He would then take great pleasure in paying everybody what he had earned.

When it came time to pay the younger helpers, he would make sure that every child understood that the amount of money received was in direct proportion to the amount of work that child had done.

"No gifts, you have earned it. It's yours," he would say.

When it came time to pay Andy, grandpa would holler his usual, "A hundred days, a hundred dollars." He would then give Andy a dollar. "You have earned it." Andy, who at eight years old was young for a regular job, had done odd jobs around the barn. He had brought sticks for the tobacco and water for the other workers. He had earned his dollar. He had never before had any money of his own, and here he was with a whole dollar in his hand. It seemed an enormous amount of money.

"When we go to the store tomorrow, you can pay for your own drink, Andy," grandpa said.

Andy just looked at his dollar.

Grandpa saw Andy's interest and continued, "You might even be able to buy a watch or a pocket knife."

Andy stared at his dollar. "Thank you, grandpa."

Grandpa hooked up his mule and cart and took eggs to the store to trade for salt, sugar, flour, and such. Andy went along.

"I believe Andy wants to buy a Pepsi," grandpa said to Mr. Greene, the store owner.

"Well, I can always use one more customer," Mr. Greene said to Andy. "What will you have?"

"I'd like a Pepsi Cola," Andy said boldly as he pulled his dollar from his trousers.

"Where did such a young fellow get so much money?" asked Mr. Greene.

"I worked for it," Andy replied. "I cleaned up around the barn and made sure everyone had water and sticks."

"That's a mighty important job. How did he handle it, Rob?" Mr. Greene asked grandpa.

"Handled it well. Did a real fine job. I got a good day's work for my dollar," grandpa replied.

"Want a piece of candy to go with that, Andy?" Mr. Greene said as he took the dollar.

Andy looked at grandpa.

"It's your dollar," grandpa said. "Spend it any way you want."

"I'll have a Baby Ruth."

"Your change is 90 cents," Mr. Greene said as he counted the money to Andy.

Andy was beaming as he consumed his drink and candy.

As they left the store, grandpa asked Andy, "Why do you think you enjoyed your drink and candy today?"

Grandpa had grown accustomed to Andy's pace and waited.

After one mile of grandpa's driving, not a sound but the hoofs of the mule on the ground and the squeaking of the cart wheels, and ten minutes of Andy's thinking, Andy said, "I enjoyed this drink and candy because I paid for it myself."

Grandpa smiled. "Work, Andy. Pay your own way through life and you'll always feel better about yourself."

Grandpa loved to teach.

After four weeks of working one day per week, Andy had four dollars less 40 cents which was the price of four Pepsi Colas and four Baby Ruths he had paid for himself. He carefully kept the change in his pocket and the bills in an old wallet given to him by grandpa.

One day the wallet slipped from Andy's trousers. Grandpa found the wallet in the front yard. He couldn't let an opportunity to teach slip by and he kept the money. Andy finally discovered his loss and came to grandpa.

"I've lost my money, grandpa." Andy said stoically.

Grandpa could see that Andy was disappointed. Knowing how much Andy enjoyed paying his own way and that the money represented Andy's life's savings, grandpa appreciated the stoicism.

"You're taking it mighty well. Do you think you'll be able to get along without it?"

"I don't have any choice, grandpa. It's gone."

Grandpa was surprised at Andy's realism but only a little surprised. He had noticed that Andy didn't seem to need too much teaching. He did a good job of figuring things out for himself.

"Well, you're no worse off now than you were four weeks ago. You were broke then. You're broke now. Do you think you can start over?"

"I don't have much choice, grandpa. It's gone."

"What about buying your own Pepsi Cola and Baby Ruth this week?"

"I'll just have to wait until I get paid again."

"Andy, you're going to be all grown up before you know it. You may have a lot of money. You may not have much money. If you have a lot or if you have a little, you're still Andy. Don't let money get close to you. It appears that you know that. I'm just saying it now so that you can remember later on when the amount may be much more than the three dollars you lost."

Grandpa took the lost wallet from his pocket and handed it to Andy. "I found it in the front yard."

"You had it all along?" said Andy, obviously pleased.

"Yes, but I thought our little discussion should come before I returned it."

Andy thought for some time. "You're right, grandpa. I'll remember what you said."

Summers at his grandparents also included grandpa's weekly Saturday trips to town for groceries. Saturday matinees with popcorn and a drink were grandpa's treat for Andy while grandpa talked politics on the street corners. Grandma cooked pound cakes, which she could do in lickety-split fashion. She also became Andy's banker after the lost wallet incident.

Summers were good. His grandparents' nineteenth century lifestyle accommodated Andy's pace beautifully. As Andy grew, he also learned that grandpa was a giant of a man in more ways than one.

THE LEGACY

Yesteryear is no bastard;
Its lineage is no game,
A pedigree without question;
And it assigns to life a name.

Hordes have gone before,
And wrestled self to knees,
For consensus gained by toil,
On the cost of victory.

A fountain of ageless wisdom,
Posterity's legacy,
Dammed for usurpation,
If it thoughtfully drinks of thee.

ANDY'S SISTER

Andy sat with his brother, Dean, just outside the kitchen on the floor and listened as his mom and Peachie talked in subdued tones. Peachie came over when Bess needed a babysitter. Andy was worried. Faye, Andy's sister, was in the children's hospital in Wilmington.

"I don't know how long you'll need to stay, Peachie. Faye is very sick. Alf is with her now. We'll both stay at the hospital until she recovers. I appreciate you coming."

"I'll stay as long as you need me. Andy and Dean will be fine. What do the doctors say?"

"They think she has rheumatic fever," Bess continued.

"Is it fatal?" Peachie asked.

"Not usually. But her temperature is extremely high, dangerously high. They are giving her aspirin and she's packed in ice and water some of the time. The fever may weaken her heart."

"Doesn't sound good."

Andy hid his face between his knees. He was really worried now.

"Alf and I will be in and out. We'll keep you informed. Just look after Andy and Dean."

"Don't worry about a thing. It will be alright around here."

Bess hugged Andy and Dean and left for the hospital. "Be good boys while I'm gone. Do everything Peachie tells you to do."

Andy watched solemnly as she drove away. "Miss Peachie, is Faye going to be alright?"

"Certainly she will," she said, trying to appear confident.

Andy could detect some doubt. "Is she going to die?"

"Certainly not." Peachie sounded more confident.

He felt a little better, but he understood Faye was seriously sick. "What happens if she dies?"

"She will go to heaven with all good boys and girls. But don't you worry about that."

"Where is heaven, Peachie?"

"You're asking some hard questions, Andy. It's a good place. People will not be sick there."

Peachie cooked, kept house, washed clothes, and looked after Andy and Dean for a week. Her lemon pies were the best Andy had ever tasted.

The news seemed to get better as the week went by and that made the pies taste even better. Finally Faye was allowed visitors, but not children. So Andy and Dean had to climb the fire escape ladder to the window of Faye's room and talk to her through the open window. Faye smiled, and Andy was finally assured that she would be okay. It was a good feeling after a week with his stomach in knots. It was a real good feeling when she finally came home. However, Andy did think that Bess's instructions that Faye was entitled to preferential treatment lasted long after Faye had fully recovered.

Rheumatic fever is also called the St. Vitus dance because of the involuntary movements of the arms, legs, and facial muscles which lasts for some period of time after the fever disappears. Faye would often appear to be dancing while standing still. She endured the teasing about such 'dancing' good-naturedly.

"Faye, you're a little out of time with the music. Try to keep up."

Faye smiled.

There was a hand-operated water pump in the back yard. It often needed priming before it produced its water flow.

"Faye," Andy called, "come grab hold of this pump handle while I pour water to start it. You won't even have to pump, just hold on."

Faye smiled. She was a good sister. And she did fully recover with no heart damage. She would grow up, marry a hard-working fellow from Chinquapin, and have a nice family. If anyone needed help, Faye was available.

The crisis was Andy's first encounter with the idea of death. He began to try and understand the process.

THE OFFER

He offered me a trip,
To which I made reply,
Maybe yes and maybe no,
Kindly tell me why.

All your friends are coming,
Some have gone before,
And you may rest assured,
All are held in store.

All my friends can wait,
I'm happy where I stand,
To leave's an inconvenience,
It's just not in my plans.

Your ticket has been ordered,
All enter by this door.
Your place is held in reserve,
And for you I do no more.

Your breath's as cold as winter,
I shiver to the spine.
And why do you wear black,
And your countenance so unkind?

Though I am most unsightly,
My appearance not the best,
I offer my assistance;
This is my sorrowful task.

But dark is all I see,
And to make this lonely trek,
Just you and me alone,
And no one ventures back.

I promise you a Light,
Much brighter that the sun,
And sights so marvelous,
Closed eyes desire to shun.

I am still reluctant,
Though if what you say is true;
You have lost your stench,
And I feel that I must too.

This argument is over;
I'll pick you up, just wait.
You must be fully dressed;
You may not at all be late.

I called after him,
As he slipped away,
How can I prepare?
You did not set the day.

DOONSIE

Doonsie was initially a neighborhood mongrel. Everyone thought he belonged to someone else. It was common to hear someone say, "I thought he was your dog." He had short legs like a dachshund, black and tan hair like a German shepherd, a head like a beagle, and the heart of a lion. Although he weighed only 40 pounds, he would fight any dog that needed fighting. Most yard dogs would let him pass unimpeded with his head in the air as if he were royalty. His pedigree, however, was never in doubt. He had none.

Anyone within a two-mile radius might wake up one morning with Doonsie on his steps for a visit. He liked people. He would spend a while, mooch a meal, and then move on. No one ever planned to feed Doonsie, but he was well nourished. At picnics or family cookouts he could charm anyone out of his last hot dog.

He became Andy's dog.

Andy spent much of his time hunting, fishing, and exploring, and Doonsie enjoyed tagging along. Doonsie soon learned when Andy's school bus would arrive, and he was there everyday at the appropriate time ready to accompany Andy anywhere. They were pals.

Doonsie saved Andy from many snake bites. On one occasion Andy was standing in a stream fishing when a water moccasin came floating along from behind Andy. Doonsie jumped in the water and was immediately on the attack. The snake was the loser. On another occasion they were walking along a narrow path. With just a couple of steps separating Andy from a rattler he did not see, Doonsie jumped in his way and upon the snake. Another snake bit the dust. Once Andy was hunting and walking up a ditch at night without his flashlight on. He heard a commotion just ahead and switched on his light. Doonsie and another water moccasin were going at it. Had it not been for Doonsie, Andy would have surely stepped directly on the snake in the narrow ditch.

Doonsie twice paid the price for his aggressive attitude toward snakes. After both snake bites his head was twice its normal size for a couple of weeks. He walked around, shaking his sore head and gingerly scratching. However, he survived with no apparent lasting effect.

His sense of direction was uncanny. When Andy became disoriented in the woods, he could turn to Doonsie and say with a wave of his hand, "Go home." Doonsie would, with Andy following. Doonsie accompanied Alvin, Andy's uncle, and Andy to Rocky Mount to look at some hunting dogs Alvin was interested in. Now, Rocky Mount is about l00 miles from Richlands. When they were part way home, they missed Doonsie. Returning to Rocky Mount, they failed to find him. They reluctantly went home and waited. Five days later Doonsie trotted in. His toenails were worn from his travels, but he was in great shape. Everyone figured he had probably put his mooching skills to good use and survived in style.

Whatever the activity, Doonsie was directly in the middle. If hogs were to be loaded for carrying to market, Doonsie 'helped'. Many pigs had heard his barking close behind and felt a nip at their rear. Of course Doonsie would be thrown paws over head a few times by hogs twenty times his weight, but he never quit 'helping'.

If there was a baseball game, he 'helped' the fielders. No amount of scolding could force him to just watch. He would momentarily lie down, but the excitement would become too much. He had to be restrained. It was just his nature to participate.

Foremost, he was Andy's friend. Andy found it easier to talk to Doonsie than to people. Doonsie would always listen. He never rushed Andy. Any pace which satisfied Andy was acceptable. If Andy was sad, Doonsie was sad. If Andy was glad, Doonsie was glad. In the quiet, solitary places around home, Andy would talk to Doonsie about everything. It was therapeutic. Their 'conversations' helped Andy to crystallize his thinking and formulate his ideas. After a quiet 'conversation' with Doonsie, Andy knew what he thought and why.

Doonsie just enjoyed being with Andy.

THE PHILOSOPHER UNCLE

Alvin was Andy's uncle. Alvin had been in the big war, World War II. While Alvin was in France, an artillery shell had exploded within a few feet of him. The explosion tore away part of Alvin's hip. He was permanently hampered with a limp. The explosion also rattled his brain. Everyone said the closed head injury made a different man of Alvin. He certainly was unique.

When Alvin reached maximum recovery from his injuries and was released from the army, he returned home with a 60% disability pension. He used the pension and his wits to support himself for the remainder of his life. He purchased a dilapidated cabin and six acres of land along the river and, with few repairs, moved in to live out his life alone.

The porch on the cabin sagged on one end. There was a squeaky swing with some of the slats missing on the other end. The doors and windows would never close completely since the house had settled unevenly. When the wood fire in his heater burned out at night in the winter, it was as cold inside as outside. There was no inside toilet. A collapsing, decaying privy was located twenty-five yards behind the house. An old pack house and crib were another fifty yards away.

His water source was a hand pump in the back yard and the river which was fed by overflows. A toothbrush, a small round mirror, and a razor for shaving hung on nails in a nearby tree. Alvin shaved every day. Andy assumed it was just something to fill his day or a habit from his army days.

Alvin did most of his cooking in the yard on an open grate surrounded by bricks. He owned one frying pan and a cauldron suspended with bailing wire over an almost continuously burning fire. It was located under a shelter which also covered his water pump. Only the very foolish, or the very brave, or Andy would partake of the cauldron's contents. It usually contained a two-or-three-day-old simmering soup made of opossum, fish, or venison or some turnips from Alvin's garden - or whatever. He cleaned his frying pan and cauldron by taking some of the sand from the river bank and scrubbing until they shined. A quick rinse under the hand pump or in the river and he was ready to start a new batch of - whatever.

His monthly shopping list included a ten-pound box of dried sausage, a 24-can box of pork and beans, salt, corn meal, and flour. These were supplements for what he could hunt down, fish out of the river, or raise himself.

Access from Haw Branch Road was along a one-half mile cart path by the river. The cart path was barely wide enough for a vehicle to pass. Bushes and overhanging trees would brush the sides of Alvin's pickup truck each time he traveled the path. Across the back window of his bright red truck hung a hunting rifle, which he actually used for hunting.

Alvin's six acres were cleared except for three shade trees around the cabin. The trees were big water oaks. He would raise turnips, cabbage, collards, cucumbers, okra, butter beans, squash, cantaloupes, and watermelons each summer on a one-half acre garden. The remainder of the six acres was a pasture which nourished a milk cow and a calf. The calf would be sold when it reached marketable size. Bantam chickens were all over.

Ten dog houses were spaced around the cabin under the shade trees. Three to ten black and tan or bluetick hound dogs usually announced the arrival of visitors, including any four legged ones, which might wonder in. Alvin always had one dog named Boss, Willie Edgar, or Blue. He trained his hunting dogs well and would often sell one for top dollar. He would never sell Boss which was always his favorite and the one which would be used to teach all of the other dogs.

All of Alvin's waking hours were spent on the necessities of life - food, clothes, shelter, and obtaining enough money to take care of those necessities. His conversation usually reflected only those concerns. Abstract ideas seemed foreign to him. Any verbal response was immediate and seemed programmed. If there was any thought behind any response, it was not evident. He was robotic. His always-brief answers did on occasion suggest that sometime in the past, probably before his war injury, he had done some amount of thinking.

For totally different reasons, Andy's and Alvin's pace of conversation was similar. Andy was slow because he thoroughly exhausted all possible avenues of thought before speaking. Alvin was quiet because of his war injury. He initiated hardly any conversation without provocation. They could be together all day with no more than ten words between them.

Andy would visit Alvin for extended periods. He liked the hunting, fishing, and swimming in the river. The solitude of the cabin retreat suited Andy just fine. There was plenty of time for thought.

A COWARD?

The task may be so menial,
That reluctance spawned of fear,
Is little but a bother,
Valor's portrait is not smeared.

The bugler's call to arms,
May not be of certain sound,
And leave a doubting soldier,
His own enlistment to command.

When my honor is assailed,
And I in haste retreat,
Take me not to task,
For something quite so cheap.

But if the clarion cry of conscience,
Dictates duty and I flee,
Or is silenced by my fright,
Then a coward I must be.

THE SWIMMING HOLE
(Growing Pains)

About l50 yards down river from the place where the river, the cart path leading to Alvin's cabin, and the paved road (Haw Branch Road) intersected, was a swimming hole. It was called Jack Island. It was not a large swimming hole, but there was enough water for cooling one's self after a hot day in the tobacco patch. Snakes often had to be ejected before humans could enter. The swimming hole was fed by cool springs, and the river at that point, which was not otherwise very deep, flowed over an outcropping of rocks causing a wash when a 'fresh' would come. A 'fresh' was just a big rain-swollen river. The wash was Jack Island. It was a favorite summer place for local youngsters. A bathing suit was not necessarily required. Water tag and follow-the-leader off the diving board were favorite games.

During one game of tag, Ronnie ran off through the bushes surrounding Jack Island to avoid being tagged only to run into a wasp hive. He ran to get into the water with wasps in pursuit. All of the other boys ran to get away from Ronnie. Five wasps won the race with Ronnie. Jack Island was full of faces just above water, noses gasping for air, and everyone beating off wasps with flicks of water until they gave up their pursuit.

Jack Island was the place where grandpa always constructed his diving board. After poles were buried in the river bank and the board attached and anchored, grandpa would be the first to dive. If it supported his 235-pound frame, it was safe for everyone else. He made it a grand spectacle. He would first walk carefully out to the end and bounce a few times. He would then retreat to the bank, get a good running start, let out a yell, make one good bounce at the end, and splash most of the water out of Jack Island. He considered a proper dive to be one where his buttocks touched the overhanging branches at the top of his dive and water splashed on the opposite bank. All of the youngsters would then join in.

Andy learned to swim and dive at Jack Island. The swimming was easiest. Diving took some effort. Andy's approach was his usual calculated effort. 'Slow' would also be a description. He would gingerly walk to the end of the board and attempt to visualize his forthcoming effort. He would bounce a few times and return to the bank.

"Go ahead, Andy, bust it open. You can do it," grandpa said encouragingly but not demandingly. He always waited for Andy.

The other boys were not so kind.

"Andy's scared," one would say.

"Give him time, boys," grandpa ordered. "He'll jump."

"It'll take him all day. We'll be gone by then," another said.

"Be patient," said grandpa.

One boy after another would push Andy aside and dive in.

Andy never had any doubt he would jump. However, he would perform no act before its time. He just ignored their jeering and concentrated on the task at hand. But he did wonder. Would his foot slip on the wet board? Would his head hit the bottom if his dive was too deep? Would a belly-flop hurt?

Finally, he had the problem solved and, to grandpa's delight, he jumped in.

"Nice dive, Andy. Do it again," grandpa said.

Andy did. Over and over again. Andy then took his turn in line to dive. He learned to dive almost as high as grandpa could, but he maintained his pace.

"Hurry, Andy," one would say.

"Move along, Andy," another ordered.

"Just a little faster," another would plead.

During the latter part of Andy's third summer of using Jack Island, a really big 'fresh' came. A hurricane blew through. The swirling water was up to the river bridge. Water, which was usually a couple of feet deep, was now ten feet of churning 'fresh'. It presented a challenge which grandpa couldn't resist. Off the river bridge he went, into the swirling waters. He swam down stream through tangled limbs and vines to Jack Island. A walk back to the bridge was followed by another swim to Jack Island.

If grandpa had any reservations about encouraging Andy to make the somewhat dangerous l50-yard swim, he did not show it. Becoming a 'man' was tops on his agenda for any youngster. Grandpa wanted any child to push himself, to accept any challenge.

"Do you want to try it, Andy?"

Andy began his calculations. Vines and logs in the way. Swirling water. Probably some snakes around. If you missed the banks of Jack Island, the river disappeared into the woods for its trip to Alvin's cabin.

"I'll walk along the bank and keep an eye on you, Andy," grandpa encouraged.

After more calculating, Andy stood on the bridge railing. A few more calculations and he jumped in. The fast-running waters began at once to carry him downstream. There was no way to swim back upstream to the bridge. Because just swimming against the current took great effort, Andy continued downstream. The current washed him into a vine-covered log. Andy pulled himself onto the log so that he could jump off the other side. When he jumped, his foot became entangled in a vine. With his foot in the vine, Andy was bobbing in the current like a cork on the end of a fishing line with its hook snagged on the river bottom. His head came to the surface only long enough for a breath of air. As he tried to turn around and free his foot with his hands, the water washed over his face. He began to choke. The underbrush along the river bank, covered in water, prevented grandpa from coming to Andy's aid.

"Hang in there, Andy," he said with growing concern. "I'll go back to the bridge and swim to you."

Andy could say nothing. He kept trying to free his foot while trying not to swallow water.

Grandpa returned to the bridge and jumped in. When he arrived at the log where Andy had been entangled, Andy was not in sight.

"Andy!" he called. "Andy!" he hollered. "Where are you?"

No answer.

Grandpa had no choice but to continue downstream, searching for Andy as he went. No Andy. Finally, when grandpa reached Jack Island, he discovered Andy standing on the bank coughing, but otherwise uninjured from his ordeal.

A relieved grandpa said as calmly as he could, "Looks like you got loose by yourself."

"I finally got loose," Andy said.

Grandpa climbed out of the water, he put his arm around Andy, and they walked back to the bridge together.

"I was sure you could do it," grandpa said proudly.

"I thought I could too, grandpa."

After the 'fresh', Jack Island was three feet wider on both sides. The dirt around one of the overhanging tree's roots had been washed away, and the following year, the tree had fallen half-way down across Jack Island at a 45-degree angle. It formed a natural diving platform at the point where its limbs were located. This platform was l5 feet high and extended over the middle of Jack Island.

As usual, grandpa was the first to take the plunge. When grandpa splashed into the water, the accumulated leaves and sediment from the bottom would churn to the top of the water. Grandpa had hit the bottom with his hands. No harm was done, and other boys began to take the plunge with more leaves and sediment appearing.

At first, Andy stayed away from the fallen tree. When he did climb to the platform, he was unable to jump. Fear? Maybe. But he had just never had time to consider all of the possibilities if he did jump. He would not jump before sufficient thought. During the tag games when he was 'it', other boys had learned that they could simply climb the tree, and when Andy would begin to climb after them, they could jump into the water leaving Andy unable to catch them.

On one occasion, the tag game ended with Andy on the platform and everyone encouraging him to jump. He waited. Everyone began leaving, muttering that Andy wouldn't jump.

Everyone except Andy and Norman had left. Norman was swimming. Andy was perched on the platform, deciding how, or if, to proceed.

"Andy, I've got a cramp," Norman called out.

"Can you still swim?" Andy responded.

"I don't think so!" Norman hollered.

And with that, Norman disappeared below the water's surface. Andy's mind began racing. To climb back down was awkward and would have taken too much time. Norman was gone. Nothing to do but dive in after him. In less than five seconds, Andy did. The battle was not over. Norman had to be found beneath the surface. Andy did and dragged Norman to the river bank.

Both boys were exhausted as they lay on the bank. Norman was coughing and spitting water.

"You saved my life, Andy," Norman said after catching his breath. "I still can't bend my leg."

"Just rest awhile. You'll be okay," said Andy.

"You jumped in after me, didn't you?"

"I guess I did," Andy said forgetting that he had jumped from the platform.

When Norman had recovered, he said, "I'm going home, Andy. Thanks again for pulling me out."

His departure left Andy and Doonsie on the bank. Andy thought about what had happened. "You know, Doonsie, I was a little afraid to jump before Norman got into trouble. When I saw Norman in trouble, I had to jump."

Andy thought some more.

Doonsie paid attention.

"I think I considered it a little foolhardy to jump when it would be easy to fall awkwardly or hit the bottom and break your neck. We don't want to be foolhardy. We don't want to be a coward either. Then too, as grandpa would say, we want to be a man. It's all a part of growing up."

Andy continued his evaluation.

"Being afraid is not being a coward. I jumped even though I was afraid."

Doonsie listened.

Andy climbed to the platform again, took the time he needed, was careful, planned his jump, and did jump - ten times. In the future when he was 'it', the platform would not be a haven for the other boys.

THE OWNER?

Toby was the neighborhood braggart. He hunted and had as many dogs as Alvin. He cherished his reputation as a hunter and spent more time by the potbelly heater at the local general store talking about hunting than he did hunting.

When he arrived at the store, the first to see him would announce, "Here's ole Toby, boys."

"Oh boy," was the chorus reply from the crowd.

"Got three last night in less than an hour," Toby said. "Ole Teeter treed in less than ten minutes."

No one paid much attention since he was as likely to be spinning yarns as telling the truth.

"Traded pickups yesterday. V8 engine. Four wheel drive. Bright blue."

A collective, "Yeah sure," could be heard from any of the crowd who might be in the store. Toby had more money, which was inherited, than common sense. He traded pickups every year anyway, and no one wanted to hear his bragging.

"Put some wood in the heater, Toby," someone said in what was a vain attempt to get Toby to be quiet.

Andy was spending time with Alvin when Toby came by one night. He wanted to go hunting as usual. In spite of all of Toby's money and efforts, Alvin's dogs were always the better dogs. Alvin spent time with his dogs. Toby's dogs were possessions.

"Howdy, Alvin, Andy. How are things going?"

"Evening, Toby," Alvin responded.

Andy nodded.

"Nice evening to go hunting," Toby suggested.

Alvin said nothing, looked around, and took a deep breath. He was smelling, evaluating the night. If he agreed with Toby's assertion, it was not obvious from his countenance.

"I expect Teeter could strike and tree a 'coon before your Blue dog could get out of the pickup," Toby continued.

Alvin walked over to his pump shelter and pulled his boots down from the nails where they were hanging. He began slowly to put them on.

"We could go over to the Lee woods. Always plenty of 'coons there," Toby said as he restlessly shifted his weight from one foot to the other, while leaning against his pickup.

"Let's go, Andy," Alvin said as he walked over to Blue and snapped a leash to his collar. He put Blue in the back of Toby's pickup with Teeter. The dogs growled nervously at each other. After some scolding, they settled down. Doonsie rode in the cab of the pickup, lying at Andy's feet. They all drove over to the Lee woods with Toby talking about anything which came to mind. Alvin said little. Andy said nothing.

"Nice weather we been having," Toby would say.

Only a nod from Alvin. Andy sat quietly.

"Can you believe the price of fur these days? It's going out of sight," said Toby.

"Yep."

The Lee woods were thick with underbrush. Fire lanes cut by the Forest Service and old logging roads made them accessible. Toby was right about one thing. There were plenty of 'coons in this thicket. Tracks were everywhere.

"Hold the dogs," Toby said as they were unloaded from the pickup. "Don't give one a head start." He was excited.

On Andy's count of three the dogs were released. Doonsie joined in, but his legs were just too short and his nose was not sensitive enough. He was not competitive and soon returned to Andy's side.

They waited quietly and listened through the night sounds for that first bark indicating a strike. After about ten minutes Blue's wailing could be heard.

"Teeter! You sorry rascal," said Toby disappointedly. "He may be lying," he suggested hopefully.

In five more minutes Blue had treed. They beat their way through the bushes to Blue. Toby called Teeter, and he joined Blue's barking up the tree. Two red eyes reflecting in the flashlight beam verified a legitimate tree. They did not take the 'coon since they were just sporting on this night.

Toby scolded Teeter. "Teeter! Where were you this time? Just loafing around, I suppose?"

Not much was said as they walked back to the truck. Toby could be heard muttering, "Stupid, lazy dog."

"Let's drive over to the north side and try again," Toby said.

"Okay," Alvin agreed.

After a similar result with Blue striking and treeing first, they returned home without conversation. Toby just muttered. The radio made the awkward silence bearable for Andy.

Toby let Alvin, Blue, Andy, and Doonsie out of the truck. As Alvin was removing Blue from Toby's truck, his belt buckle scratched the side of Toby's brand new, blue truck.

Alvin simply said, without emotion, "Sorry."

Toby said, "Never mind." He tried to wipe off the scratch and was obviously distressed.

Andy wondered if the scratch was intentional.

When leaving, Toby turned to Alvin and said, "I'll give you $500.00 for Blue."

"We'll talk about it. Time to go to bed tonight."

Toby left in a huff.

Alvin just smiled at Andy as Toby drove away. Andy could not determine the reason for Alvin's smile. Was he satisfied by the hunt's results? Did he think Toby was funny? One never knew about Alvin.

Early the next morning Toby appeared again. Alvin was shaving at his mirror on the tree. "I'll give you $l,000.00 for that dog."

After what seemed to Toby an eternity, Alvin said, "Give me a couple of days to think about it."

Toby left in another huff.

Exactly two days later Toby returned. "Well? What about it?"

Alvin was feeding his dogs and continued without responding.

"Alvin, are you going to sell me that dog or not?"

Another delayed response. "I've had Blue for two years, since he was a pup. Give me a couple more days."

"I'll give you $2,000.00 cash today," Toby pressed on.

Alvin finally turned to Andy and said, "Get Blue for me, Andy."

A big smile crossed Toby's face as he watched Andy put Blue in the back of his pickup. He counted twenty $l00.00 bills and gave them to Alvin. He was obviously excited as he drove away.

"He would have paid more," Alvin said.

"Why didn't you wait for more?" Andy questioned.

"Two thousand dollars was enough. No need to steal from a fool just because you can," Alvin said as he ambled over to the bricks around his grate. He removed a loose brick which exposed a hiding place. He took out a jar, screwed off the top, placed the $2,000.00 inside, and returned the lid and jar to their hiding place. Andy noticed some money already in the jar.

As Alvin walked off to finish feeding his dogs, he said partly to Andy and partly to himself, "The dog owns Toby."

Andy was surprised. The statement indicated some thought by Alvin so Andy questioned, "What do you mean, Alvin?"

Alvin simply repeated, "The dog owns Toby."

Andy had learned that when Alvin repeated himself, he did not discuss the matter further. It was as if by some mysterious means, even to Alvin himself, he had reached his decision and it was final. Alvin seemed not to be able to repeat the thought processes used to make his decision. No amount of persuasion would elicit further conversation or change his mind. If he repeated something a third time, he was clearly agitated.

After they had finished feeding all of the dogs, Andy took Doonsie down to the river's edge and sat down. He threw pebbles and sticks into the water to watch the ripples. He thought about Toby, Alvin, Blue, and the sale for $2,000.00.

He finally asked Doonsie, "What do you think, Doonsie? Does Blue own Toby?"

Doonsie waggled his tail and moved closer to Andy for a pat.

Andy patted Doonsie.

Andy had noticed the differences between Alvin and Toby. He said to Doonsie in his deliberate manner, pausing after each sentence to reflect, "Alvin was self-contained. He seemed to need nothing. He managed while Toby craved. Alvin could let Blue go even though he had owned him for two years. Toby was controlled by circumstances. The dog was his immediate concern and that concern controlled him. Alvin is right. Blue owns Toby."

Andy concluded, "Let's say it this way, Doonsie. Possessions, like a rabid dog, may turn on their owners." With that said, Andy patted Doonsie on the head and gave him some good rubs down his back.

Doonsie had assisted Andy one more time.

THE TAINTED CANDY BAR
(Growing Pains Continued)

That first bicycle really increases the size of a young boy's world. Just a few minutes of riding could put a fellow miles from home. It provided Andy with access to Mr. Green's store on a regular basis. Mr. Green's store was on the main road at the point where it connected to Haw Branch Road. Since David also had a bicycle and his house was located on the way to Mr. Green's store, David and Andy often rode together to the store. A Pepsi and Baby Ruth candy bar were the usual purchase. A dip in Jack Island on the return trip was probable in the summertime. Doonsie always tagged along with tongue dangling from his efforts to keep up with the bicycles.

"Good afternoon, boys," Mr. Green said as they peddled up. Mr. Green was in his usual position, seated in a rocking chair under the store shelter. He waved a fan in front of his face with his right hand. His right arm rested on his ample stomach. "Aren't you kind of hot riding those bicycles today?"

"A little bit," Andy said, "but we're going to jump in Jack Island on the way back home."

"That ought to cool things down a little. I expect you boys are looking for a Pepsi and a Baby Ruth."

"Mind if we put a little air in our tires before we go in, Mr. Green?" David asked.

"Go right ahead. Use all you need."

The air pump was beside the store. As they checked the pressure and pumped air into a tire, David whispered to Andy, "When we get inside, talk to Mr. Green about buying a pocket knife. You don't have to buy one. Just talk to him about it."

"Why?" questioned Andy.

"Just do what I say."

When they were inside, Mr. Green had pulled their Pepsis from the cooler and placed them on the counter. "You boys get your own candy bar. You know where they are. That will be ten cents each, boys."

They paid Mr. Green. As they opened the candy bars and began to eat, David nudged Andy and whispered, "Ask him about the pocket knives."

"No," said Andy. "I don't want a pocket knife."

"Just ask him anyway. Just talk to him about a knife."

Andy reluctantly walked to the pocket knives which were at the other end of the counter.

"Are these pocket knives any good, Mr. Green?"

"Some of the best made," Mr. Green replied. "They got a long and a short blade, and they are real sharp."

Andy could see past Mr. Green to where David was standing. Mr. Green's back was toward David.

"Keep talking," David mouthed without sound.

"Do you think they'll make a good carving knife?" Andy was nervous by now.

"I'm sure they will," Mr. Green said as he glanced over his shoulder at David.

David smiled and took a swallow of his Pepsi.

"How much are they?" Andy continued. He saw David quickly take two candy bars from the counter and cram them into his pocket.

"Two dollars and 98 cents."

"I don't have that much money right now, Mr. Green," Andy said as he quickly finished his drink and went outside. He leaned against the gas tanks. He felt sick to his stomach.

He got on his bicycle and rode off. David had to hurry to catch up.

"You didn't pay for those candy bars, did you?" Andy asked.

"I got one for you and one for me," David said, avoiding the question.

Andy was quiet as they stopped off at Jack Island for their swim. Swimming had never been so little fun.

David noticed the somber mood and was beginning to feel pangs of conscience. "I'm going on home, Andy."

David rode off leaving Doonsie and Andy behind. When he put on his shirt, he found that David had put a candy bar into his pocket.

"Oh boy, Doonsie. I knew David was up to something. What am I going to do now?"

Andy began to wrestle with his thoughts.

"I can't keep it. It's not mine."

He wrestled some more.

"If I take it back to Mr. Green, I'll have to tell on David. I'm in a mess. I was in a mess even before David put the candy in my pocket. I've got to do something."

He was searching for an answer.

"Anything will be better than this sick feeling in my stomach."

He sat by the river for thirty minutes. He pondered. He patted Doonsie. He pondered. He finally got on his bicycle and rode off to the store.

"I'd like to return this candy and I owe you for another candy bar, Mr. Green," Andy said hurriedly as he peddled up and got off his bike.

"How's that, Andy?"

"We didn't pay for two candy bars when we came earlier."

Mr. Green remembered distinctly that the boys had paid for the candy bars which they had eaten. He took note of Andy's nervous demeanor. He remembered the awkward discussion about the pocket knives. It began to make sense to him and he asked, "Andy, did you take this candy?"

"No."

"Did David take the candy?"

"Yes."

"He took the candy while you asked about the knives, didn't he?"

"Yes."

"Did you know he was going to take the candy?"

"No, but I knew he was up to something."

Mr. Green thought for some time. "Well, it took real courage to come back like this."

"I just feel sick, Mr. Green. I'm sorry."

"What do you think we should do?"

"I don't know. I'll do whatever you say."

"Well, if I take this candy back and let you pay for the missing candy, do you think you'll ever do this again?"

"I don't think so, Mr. Green."

“Got yourself into a real mess, didn’t you?" Mr. Green said after some thought.

"Yes."

"Got yourself into a mess because a friend asked you to do something wrong and you did it.” Mr. Green paused. “And when a friend asks you to do something, not only do you have to decide if it's right or wrong, you have to also decide if you're going to offend your friend by saying no. You have that added pressure.” Mr. Green paused again. “Remember, Andy, even if a friend asks you to do something wrong, you must still say no. Do you understand?"

Andy thought about what Mr. Green had said. "Yes sir, Mr. Green." He then gave Mr. Green the candy bar and five cents.

"You're still welcome in my store any time, Andy."

"Thank you, Mr. Green," Andy said with bowed head. He slowly mounted his bike and peddled off.

He had only gone a short distance when he met David.

"When you didn't come by the house, I figured you had come back here," David said. "Did you tell Mr. Green?"

"Yes."

"Everything?"

"Yes."

"What did he say?"

"You can go talk to him yourself."

Andy watched as David peddled up to the store. He watched as David and Mr. Green talked. Finally David came back.

"Mr. Green says I should give you this," David said as he gave Andy a nickel. "He also said I should tell you that I'm sorry for asking you to do something wrong."

"Are you mad, David?"

"No, I know it was wrong to take the candy and I'm sorry I asked you to help."

"No hard feelings. I should have known better myself. I don't know about you, but I feel better than I did about an hour ago," Andy said.

"Yep. I feel better. I'm never going to get myself into such a mess again."

THE DROUGHT

There was a year when there was no rain for three months. The local weather station measured .000l of an inch of rain. The weather man surmised that that drop blew in from South Carolina on the hot spring and summer winds that helped evaporate the precious little surface water that had been available. The river by Alvin's place stopped running, leaving a few deep holes where the fish collected. The springs feeding Jack Island slowed to a trickle. Jack Island was only three feet deep. The spring water could not flow down stream before it was sucked into the surrounding dry earth. Leaves and grass turned brown in the middle of summer. Corn grew to a height of two feet and curled up. Tobacco fared no better. The weather, always a topic of conversation in a farming community, dominated the discussions at the general store and barber shop.

And the drought dragged on.

Doonsie lay by the front door as Laney cut Andy's hair. Laney was the local barber.

"Do you think it'll ever rain?" Toby began.

"It'll rain. We just have to be a little patient," said Laney.

"A little patient. It's been three months," countered Toby.

"Three months ain't no long time," old man Stevens chimed in. "Back in 'l7 it didn't rain for nine months. Why, the ground was baked so hard you could go out to that old clay hill by Four Corners and carve out enough bricks to build a house."

"There ain't no clay hill at Four Corners," Toby said, leading with his chin.

"I know. We used it all up building houses," laughed Mr. Stevens.

Others joined in the laughter.

Toby huffed which caused another chorus of laughter.

"It is getting serious, though. Farmers are going to lose a lot of money this year," said Laney. "Planted all those seeds, put fertilizer in the ground, and they ain't going to get anything back."

"Sounds about like any other year to me," said Mr. Stevens. "Poor old farmer. Buys seeds and fertilizer at the seller's price, raises his crops, and then sells his crops to a buyer who also sets the price. It's a wonder they have lasted as long as they have."

"I know what you mean," Mr. Morton joined in. "You heard the story about the farmer who hit the jackpot for a $l,000,000.00, didn't you, Toby?

"No, tell me about it," Toby played along.

"Someone asked him what he was going to do with the money and he said he'd probably just keep on farming until it was gone."

Toby joined in the laughter this time. But after they had finished their laughter, all agreed that it was a serious matter and that some folks, who had not previously done so, ought to consider going to church come Sunday and to pray for rain.

When Laney had finished with Andy's haircut, Andy and Doonsie began their walk over to Alvin's place where they would spend the weekend. They surveyed the drought damage as they walked along. Andy pulled off his shoes and walked barefoot through the burned out corn fields. A long drought begins to make everyone feel uneasy. A feeling of urgency was in the air. Andy could feel the urgency.

"We need rain, Doonsie. It makes you feel like something is wrong when it doesn't rain. Nature seems to be at odds with itself."

A dust trail followed Andy and Doonsie as they walked through the fields.

Andy noticed the river had stopped running and saw the fish in the small holes gulping air from the surface in an attempt to get enough oxygen to survive. Some did not. There were some holes completely dry and with partially eaten fish all about. Raccoons and other critters had a feast with such easy pickings. Andy could do nothing but shake his head and hope the rains would soon come. It all seemed such a waste.

Alvin was seated under his shade tree with supper simmering over his open fire when Andy arrived.

"Come on up, Andy. Have a seat," Alvin smiled. That was about the extent of any of Alvin's welcomes, but Andy knew that he was welcomed. The smile was enough.

Andy walked by the boiling pot and peered in. He wasn't sure of its contents.

"What you got cooking, Alvin?"

"A fish stew. I cleaned out one of those holes in the river. Just walked in and picked 'em up. I've added some potatoes, onions, and a tomato or two. Ought to be ready in a little bit."

"Sounds good," but Andy wondered.

A couple of Alvin's dogs trotted up to Andy with a few half-hearted howls and he gave them a pat. Doonsie and the dogs smelled and circled each other for a while and finally settled down under the shade tree.

They listened to the dry, hot breezes in the trees. They listened to the birds singing. Their songs seemed stressful. A few crickets had begun to chirp. They all watched the stew cook. Alvin would keep tasting and adding this or that. Andy placed his hands behind his head and nodded.

After awhile Alvin announced, "She's ready." And he began dipping Andy's helping into his tin plate.

Andy surveyed his supper with some reservations about eating. He tasted a little portion. To his surprise, it was good and he began to eat hardily.

"Good stuff, Alvin."

Alvin smiled. He then took his own helping and poured half of the stew into a tub. "I'll let that cool and feed the dogs."

Andy and Alvin ate until they were full. Andy cooled some for Doonsie and fed him. Alvin then dumped the tub contents into five different containers for his dogs. They all wanted to eat from the first to be filled and Alvin had to part growling dogs with kicks and threats. All of the dogs were finally fed.

"Tomorrow we'll clean out that deep hole in the bend and have fried fish. Some of my cabbage filled out before the drought took effect. I'll cut one and make some slaw," Alvin said.

Everyone settled down to pick teeth and lick chops.

"What more could a man want?" Alvin finally mused.

Andy was always interested when Alvin said something like that. It certainly indicated Alvin did some thinking while living all alone. He also knew it was probably useless to try and pry into Alvin's mind. Alvin never looked back, or could not look back, into his thinking process. Andy would try notwithstanding.

"What do you mean, Alvin?"

"What more could a man want?" Alvin repeated.

Andy knew better than to ask again. But he would press on a little.

"Well, a man could want a big fine castle to live in," Andy suggested.

"Just for show," Alvin said.

"A man could want a million dollars."

"Just paper."

"A man could want fame."

"Just puffs the ego. No lasting value."

"A man could want a woman."

Alvin thought for some time but said nothing. The pace or the depth of the conversation was unusual for Alvin. He appeared exhausted. Or maybe it was the particular question. Andy asked no more. Alvin finally got up from his chair and disappeared down one of the paths leading to the river, leaving Andy with Doonsie. Andy hoped that he had not upset Alvin.

Andy was dirty from the day's activities. Dusty walks with sweat equals dirty boy. He would normally bathe in the river this time of year, but since it had stopped running, it was not so clean. He pumped one of Alvin's tubs full of water and placed it over the open fire. After the water was warm, he stood in the tub and took a bath. As he bathed, he talked with Doonsie at his comfortable pace.

"Doonsie, Alvin's right about some things. The physical body doesn't need much more than a little food. Adequate clothes. A rudimentary shelter such as Alvin's cabin over there. Anything more than that is what we want - what we set our hearts on - what satisfies our passions. I know some greedy people because they love money. I know some vain people because they love attention. I know some angry people because they cannot live with their own failures. I know some good people too. The good ones seem to be simple. They don't want too much. You can't easily offend them. I guess that's why some old sage has said we need to be careful what we set our hearts on for we shall surely obtain it."

Andy dried himself with one of Alvin's towels which had been hanging under the shelter. He washed the towel and hung it back on its nail. He rinsed his under shorts, wrung them as dry as he could and put them back on. They would be dry in just a few minutes. His shirt and trousers were washed and hung out to dry. They would also be dry in a few minutes.

Andy continued his conversation with Doonsie. "Just between you and me, Doonsie, I'm not sure if a female is a need or a want. They are sure beginning to be something pretty to me. I think about them more and more. I'll just think about that for a while - and, by the way, enjoy it." He patted Doonsie saying, "Thanks for listening."

Alvin returned just before dark. Andy had no idea where he had been.

Andy noticed a dark cloud off to the southwest and asked, "Any rain in that cloud, Alvin?"

"Nope, the air's too dry." Alvin had his mind already made up. "That cloud is like people who make promises but don't keep'em."

Andy appreciated the analogy but decided against starting another heavy conversation with Alvin. He noted that the wind kicked up, the cloud blew over in a few minutes, and there was some lightning and thunder, but no rain. Alvin was right - a promise of rain but no delivery.

And the drought dragged on.

The next day Andy and Alvin went to the deep hole in the bend of the river and gathered the fish by just reaching down into the shallow water. They had fried fish with slaw for supper.

Alvin took Andy home.

"See you next weekend," Andy said as he got out of Alvin's pickup.

"Come any time. I always like to see you come."

The drought lasted into the next weekend. Andy kept listening for rain on his roof top. But there was none. That same feeling of urgency prevailed. The earth needed rain.

Andy was at Alvin's when he saw the clouds rolling in. "Any rain in those clouds, Alvin?"

Alvin stood up excitedly. He took a deep breath. He looked all around. "I believe there is rain coming, Andy. There will be an abundance of rain. The earth will be renewed. This parched creature will revive. She will live again."

And it did rain - buckets. Neither Andy nor Alvin bothered to get under the shelter. They sat in the rain. Andy stuck his tongue out to feel it. Alvin turned his face to the rain. They were soaked. The water began to pool in low places and then run off toward the river. What a beautiful sight, thought Andy.

"Always keep your promise. Don't be a dry cloud," Alvin said.

The beauty of it all had shaken Alvin from his usually stoic posture. Andy had never seen Alvin with this much to say before. He didn't probe. He enjoyed. He would remember.

They went to bed relieved. The feeling of urgency was gone. They could rest.

The next morning was vibrant, radiant. Overnight, the grass and leaves had taken a big drink of water. The morning sparkled for the first time in months. It was as if nature were taking a relieved breath of its own. It was not at odds with itself anymore.

Over a fried-eggs-and-sausage breakfast cooked over the open fire, Alvin had one more burst of inspiration. "You know, Andy, it rains in the heart too."

Something so gentle from an otherwise tough, solitary man, Andy thought. He wanted to talk about it, but he enjoyed the morning and the renewed life all around without further conversation.

They ate in silence.

DROUGHT

The drought dragged on,
Withering and dying,
As the drought dragged on --
Advantage to the sun.

The little reserve,
A reservoir within,
Used sparingly but finally --
Consumed by the sun.

The substance of life,
Viability gone,
Now rendered hard --
Baked by the sun.

The weak fell first,
Unable to stand,
Dry said the postmortem --
Parched by the sun.

Relief from this drought,
A dearth of the heart,
Showers of love --
Subduing the sun.

BOYS' NIGHT OUT

David was three months older than Andy so he obtained his drivers license first. On the first Friday after David's l6th birthday David's dad allowed him to take the family car for a night out. He picked up Andy just before dark and off they went. *Toot and Tell It,* the local drive-in eatery, was their destination. Mildred was the carhop. A bologna-with-chili-and-slaw sandwich was the specialty. The price was fifteen cents. *Toot and Tell It* was the place to be seen in Richlands. No one who was anyone ever drove directly into a parking space. A few circles of the restaurant were mandatory - just to be seen and to see who was there. The circling would often cause bumper-to-bumper traffic jams, but no one cared. No one was going any place anyway.

"Well, look who's here," someone hollered as David and Andy circled. "Does your mommy know you're out of the house?"

David showed them his middle finger. Andy slid lower into his seat and watched. Andy was already uncomfortable.

"Oh, aren't we sassy?" someone said as the assembled crowd hooted and hollered.

David kept driving and, after circling an acceptable number of times, finally parked.

"Are you boys eating, drinking, or looking?" Mildred asked.

"Give us a beer, Mildred," David ordered.

"Now you know you're too young for that. Come back in a couple of years."

"We'll have two bologna sandwiches with chili and slaw and two Pepsis."

Andy nodded his head.

"Sounds more like it." Mildred left and returned in ten minutes with their order.

Every now and then a car would peel rubber as it left. That was often a challenge for anyone there to follow if he wanted to race.

Andy would have enjoyed eating in peace, but no such luck. They were joined by Skeeter and Lloyd. They knew David from playing on the basketball team together. They were also two years older which was old enough to drink beer. Each had a beer.

"Want a drink?" Skeeter asked.

"Yeah, give me a swallow," David said. He then gulped what was left in the can.

"Hey there. Go easy on my beer. Get Mildred out here. We need another beer."

David blinked his headlights and Mildred came.

"You boys need something?"

"Give us a couple more beers, Mildred." Skeeter said.

"You fellows aren't letting these two kids drink, are you?"

"No, nothing like that. Just give us two more beers."

"Okay, but if I catch you giving any to these kids, I'll throw you off these premises."

"Kids?" David questioned. "Just get in this car with me and I'll show you who's a kid."

"Kid is what I said and kid is what I mean."

David reached out the car and tried to grab, her but she retreated to get their order.

"You boys looking for girls?" Lloyd asked.

"Sure, ain't everybody?" David answered.

"Well, I think I know where some are." Lloyd winked at Skeeter.

"Yeah, just over the county line." Skeeter joined in. "What do you say? Want to go?"

"Just lead the way," David replied.

Andy watched and listened.

Mildred served the two beers to Skeeter and Lloyd. They finished them with David sneaking his share. They all watched the circling cars, waved to friends, and wondered aloud when a stranger passed.

"Drive on over to the county line, David." Skeeter ordered.

"Sounds like as good a place as any," David said. And off they went.

The girls' house was in the middle of nowhere. It had a big yard and six cars were parked in it. There was one light outside by the door and a neon sign in the window which said 'Open'.

"Hey. What kind of girls are these?" David questioned.

"Just keep your shirt on and wait here. I'll be right back," Skeeter said.

Andy watched as Skeeter knocked on the door. A mountain of a man cracked the door and spoke to Skeeter. They exchanged a few words, but Andy could not understand any of what they were saying.

"It's only $l0.00," Skeeter said as he returned to the car.

"Ten dollars for what?" David asked.

"Ten dollars for a good roll in the hay. What did you think I was talking about?"

"Not bad," David said nervously while trying to hide some reservations he was having.

"Andy?" Skeeter asked.

Andy had been watching so intently he was surprised to hear his name called. "I hadn't thought about it," he finally said when he had recovered.

"Well, you like girls, don't you?" Skeeter pressed on.

"Sure. But paying one? And I don't even know her."

"You don't have to know her. Just pay her. You're not scared, are you?"

"No, I'm not scared."

"You don't have the money, do you?"

Andy thought about saying no since that would get him off the hook, but he did have the money and didn't want to lie. "I have the money."

"Well, what's your problem?"

"I just haven't had time to think about it."

"Oh, come on, Skeeter," Lloyd said. "You'll be talking to him all night."

"Forget it. Just do what you want to do," Skeeter said as they left.

Andy was relieved when all three went inside while he waited in the car. He was uneasy with the situation. He just watched and waited and thought about what was going on inside. He would talk with Doonsie about it when he got home.

They finally returned. David was all smiles. They laughed and joked about the encounter all the way back to *Toot and Tell It.* Skeeter and Lloyd got out and went to their own cars. The mood was somewhat sober as David and Andy returned home.

"Why didn't you go in, Andy?" David asked.

"I reckon I just didn't want to bad enough."

"You don't think bad of me because I did, do you?"

"That's not for me to say, David."

"I can tell. You think I shouldn't have done it."

"I don't know, David. Just make up your own mind about it."

"To tell the truth, I feel kind of like I did after I took the candy bar from Mr. Greene and I don't know why."

"You'll figure it out," Andy said as he got out of the car at his home.

Doonsie was lying on the porch and jumped up to meet Andy. Andy's mother came to the door to see who was there.

"Is that you, Andy?"

"Yes, Mom. I'm going for a walk with Doonsie. I'll be back in a few minutes."

"Okay, but don't be long. It's kind of late."

He walked along the edge of the fields with Doonsie. Doonsie seemed to know that it was time for a talk and put on his listening face.

"Doonsie, I could have had a girl for $l0.00." After some more thought he said, "Let me rephrase that. I could have had a girl's body for $l0.00. Big difference there, don't you think? Of course, I must admit that having a girl's body has its appeal, but...."

Andy thought some more. "If $l0.00 is all it's worth, it ain't worth very much."

Andy thought some more. "If the girl wants only me, then that would be priceless. You couldn't buy that with a king's ransom. The king, himself, could not decree it and make it so. Now, Doonsie, that has more appeal. It is beautiful. It seems almost sacred. It warms the heart instead of just exciting the body."

Andy thought some more.

"Take my word for it, Doonsie, the body is excited easily enough. Matters of the heart take longer. You must search for them amid exciting distractions."

Andy thought some more.

"I think the bottom line is this, Doonsie. I'm a one-woman-man searching for a one-man-woman."

Andy and Doonsie began their walk back home. Just before they arrived, Andy said, "Doonsie, the exciting part can be very demanding. You stay here." Andy walked off by himself.

SEARCHING

Christened and then launched,
No baggage in tow,
The search begins in earnest;
The call is to go.

An obscure aching,
Will not be ignored,
Enticing and persistent,
To see the other shore.

No effort is spared;
Obstacles are no bar;
All's directed and focused,
To reach for distance star.

So enchanting is its lure,
Caution's thrown to wind,
Pursuit at any cost,
Just to find rainbow's end.

Lest the chase be in vain,
And a mirage at journey's end,
Focus at the turnstile,
Restless heart's wayward aim.

EMILY IN HIGH SCHOOL

By the time Emily reached high school, she had learned to cope with her shyness. However, a flushed face was the standard response to the sound of her name being called or learning that she was the center of attention. She had trained herself to wait for the initial shock to subside. She could then function normally. She had also learned to shorten the waiting period. Looking into people's eyes took some effort. She was more comfortable alone than in a crowd.

Everything did not always proceed smoothly.

The high school students had gathered in the auditorium for assembly. Assembly was a weekly gathering of the entire high school student body when the principal would stand before everyone and act like a principal. He would make any announcement he felt necessary, introduce new teachers, and announce the holiday schedule and all school happenings. Some class president would render a forgettable speech. The Spanish Club might inform the gathering about Spanish culture. The Glee Club might sing a song.

"Before this assembly is dismissed, Miss Emily Wheeler will present a musical rendition of the Lord's Prayer. She will accompany herself on the piano," the principal announced.

Emily's face flushed as usual. But she proceeded to the piano, took her seat, and waited for the initial shock to disappear. It didn't disappear. She played the introduction, but when it came time to sing, she couldn't. Her throat was just too full.

She played the introduction again. Same results. When it came time to sing, she couldn't. By this time the assembly was somewhat expectant. Emily took a deep breath and played the introduction again. Determined this time, she completed her presentation.

"Thank you, Miss Wheeler," the Principal announced. "This assembly is adjourned. You may return to your classes."

Emily remained seated while the auditorium cleared.

"Come on, Emily. Let's get back to class," said Betty, Emily's best friend.

"Oh, Betty. I was terrible," Emily lamented.

"What are you talking about?"

"I really blew that one."

"What are you talking about?" Betty repeated emphatically.

"Didn't you notice I had to start over three times?"

"No, I thought you did a great job."

"You didn't notice anything unusual?"

"Not at all."

"Well, I expect everyone else noticed."

"Ah, forget it. No one noticed. Let's go on to English. Mike will be there."

"Are boys all you ever think about, Betty? Honestly."

"Don't give me that, Emily. You know you think about them too."

"I didn't say I didn't, Betty. But they are not going to make a fool out of me." Emily had to admit to herself that she did think about boys a lot. But she would not swoon, giggle, and fall all over herself when they were around. Some boy would have to earn her attention and respect. She would keep her distance until then.

As they entered the English classroom, Mike came over to Betty and gave her a big kiss. Emily looked away. Betty giggled as Mike whispered something in her ear. Emily tried not to notice. They continued to whisper and flirt throughout the English period.

After class, Betty came to Emily. "Mike wants to go out Saturday. Do you want to go with us and Bert?"

"I don't know, Betty. You know I don't really fit in."

"His friend Bert needs a date. Do it for me."

"Where are you going? What are you going to do?"

"Get something to eat, hang out, you know. There's a pool party with music at Mike's. Come on."

"I don't even get along with Bert that well."

"Just this once? It's not really a date. You'll just make an even number of boys and girls."

"Okay," Emily said reluctantly.

"We'll pick you up at your house at l:00."

The pool party was about what Emily expected - loud, some drinking, with people trying hard enough to have a good time, a little too hard maybe. It was not naturally relaxing. It was not at the top of her list of ways to spend Saturday afternoon. She endured. She ate potato chips and sipped a Coke with Bert. They looked at each other and forced smiles. Both were uncomfortable.

"Want to dance?" Bert finally asked.

"This one is a little too fast, Bert. Let's wait for the next one."

Bert jumped up and grabbed Sue, and they danced. As Bert danced by Betty, he whispered, "Next time don't do me any favors. Does she even dance?"

"Go easy on her, Bert. She's a little different, the quiet type, you know," Betty answered.

They finished dancing and Bert took his seat next to Emily.

"I heard you sing at assembly on Wednesday. I thought you did a great job."

"Thank you, Bert," Emily answered. She took the opportunity to seek some assurance. "Did you notice anything unusual about my singing?"

"No. No, it was just fine."

"Well, thank you again, Bert."

After more awkward silence Bert finally said, "This one is a little slower. Want to try it?"

"Okay."

Bert tried to hold Emily close and she pulled away.

"Okay. Okay." Bert said as he held up both hands and backed off. They finished the dance and sat down.

"Bert, neither one of us is having much fun. Do you want to take me home?"

"Might as well. I'll get Mike's car keys. Be right back."

The drive to Emily's home was quiet. But as they approached the city park, Emily, not wanting the day to be a total loss, said, "Let's stop at the park and swing some, Bert."

"Swing? I haven't done that in years," Bert answered.

"Not afraid of looking silly, are you?" Emily prodded.

"No. No, I'll do it."

They swung. It was now Bert who appeared bored. Emily closed her eyes and felt the wind in her face. She felt relieved to be away from the crowd. She was now in her element.

"What do you think of tomorrow, Bert?"

"Well, tomorrow is Sunday." Bert was puzzled.

"No, no, I'm not talking about tomorrow. I'm talking about the future."

"Oh, hadn't thought much about that." After a long pause he said, "I was kind of hoping we could beat Central in basketball this year."

Emily could see that this conversation was going nowhere fast, but she pressed on.

"What about the bomb? Will humanity be here fifty years from now? Will we outgrow our food supply?"

"Heavy. Heavy. I hadn't thought about those things at all." Bert was quiet.

Emily could also see that he was not going to start thinking about those things now. She closed her eyes and again felt the wind on her face. She dreamed of a world to come and what it might hold. But mostly, she dreamed of someone, someone who would listen to her heart. Here she was in the middle of a city with

people all around and with someone next to her, and sh
lonely.

Both Emily and Bert were totally exhausted from trying to make this date bearable. Bert finally drove Emily home in total silence. Neither was sorry it was their one and only date.

"How did you date go, Emily? Aren't you home early?" asked Emily's mom as Emily came in.

"I just found out what happens when two completely different worlds collide, Mom. Disaster. Catastrophe. Chaos."

"Was it that bad, Sweetheart?"

"Worse. Is there one boy in the world who doesn't think all of the time of his car, or his hair, or a big time, or - oh yes - that number one priority - sex? Don't they care what I'm thinking? Don't they want to know how I feel? I mean, I think about sex. I look forward to it. I think it will be really nice with the right boy."

"Well, don't you mean with the right husband?"

"You know what I mean, Mom."

"I do know what you mean. And you need not worry. The right boy - let's say young man - will come along and you'll be all starry-eyed. You'll feel all giddy inside. Love does make fools of everyone so be as careful as you can. You won't be able to sleep for thinking about him. He'll be the last thing at night and the first thing in the morning you'll think about. He will be worth waiting for. So be patient."

"Sounds wonderful, Mom. And I try to be patient but I don't know. Does it really happen?" Emily asked wistfully. "Will he be tall? Will he be short? Will he be smart? What color will his eyes be?"

"It will happen. And he will be perfect, at least in your eyes. Patience is the secret."

They went to the kitchen and ate a sandwich together and talked of simple things. They baked a cake together.

As they retired to their rooms for the evening, Emily said, "Mom, I'm lucky to have you. Do you want to go and see the flowers at the state park in Goldsboro with me tomorrow?"

"Maybe."

"You know I like to go there in the spring. It's already a little late this year, but there will be some flowers still in bloom."

"We'll talk about it in the morning. Sweet dreams."

IDENTICAL TEST SCORES

Mrs. Oates was Andy's ninth grade teacher for homeroom, math, and English. The subjects were an odd combination, to be sure, but teachers in small schools often taught courses out of their field. She normally taught English.

Mrs. Oates was partial to quiet children. She and Andy were natural kindred spirits. They liked each other. If she had a pet, it was Andy. If Andy could talk to any teacher, it was Mrs. Oates.

There was an occasion when Mrs. Oates assigned to the class a poem to memorize by the following week. Andy knew who would be the first called upon to recite the poem. He was ready. He recited all one hundred lines without a mistake. Knowing that he had done so, but looking for approval from Mrs. Oates, he returned to his seat by way of her desk to watch her enter his grade. She feigned hiding her grade book while leaving an unobstructed view for Andy to see her enter a grade of l00.

She would often offer Andy's work to the class as an example. The class noticed the special relationship. No one objected because Mrs. Oates had a knack, developed over her years of teaching, for making all of her students feel good about themselves. She praised when praise was due. She gently corrected when correction was due.

There was also an occasion in an English class where the characters in a play hugged each other. A question arose during discussion by the class about the kind of hug that had occurred. After some zealous student suggest that Mrs. Oates and Andy demonstrate the hug, the whole class chimed in, suggesting they should. They did.

Their special relationship survived one small bump in the road. It did not seem so small to Andy.

Theresa, a classmate, sat directly across the aisle from Andy. During a math test she began to try and look at Andy's answers.

Andy initially positioned his paper out of Theresa's view and continued his work. He would forget to position his paper and Theresa would again look. Finally, he allowed her to look. They completed the test. But the incident was far from over. Andy could not eat lunch. He could not concentrate for the remainder of the day. He found sleeping difficult that night.

At the next math class, Mrs. Oates distributed the test papers and discussed the correct answers with the class. She then collected the students' papers.

"Andy? Theresa? I need to speak with you," she said as the class ended.

The other students filed from the classroom.

"I noticed that the two of you made exactly the same grade on this test. Your answers to each of these problems are exactly the same. Do you have an explanation?"

Neither said anything.

She asked them directly, "Did you two cheat on this test?"

After an agonizing delay while looking down at her feet, Theresa said, "No."

Andy didn't want to hurt Theresa and responded more quickly than he usually did and without much thought, "I didn't do anything Mrs. Oates". His attempted rationalization and justification didn't accomplish its purpose. Even as he finished his denial he felt as if a dagger had pierced his chest.

Mrs. Oates said nothing. After a thoughtful delay and piercing stares, she dismissed them, "You may go."

Andy and Theresa walked out the door and down the hall without a word. It was another long, sleepless night for both of them. The next morning before class they talked about how terrible they had felt all night.

"What a night," said Theresa.

"I didn't sleep a wink last night either," Andy agreed.

More silence.

Finally Andy said, "We have to tell Mrs. Oates."

Theresa reluctantly agreed, "Yes."

The math class finally cleared of other students leaving Andy, Theresa, and Mrs. Oates. Mrs. Oates appeared to be grading papers for ten minutes without saying a word. She was actually turning up the temperature in the room. Every couple of minutes she would look over her glasses at Andy and Theresa. Andy and Theresa sat quietly but restlessly. Did the seats actually feel hot? Was the temperature in the room l00 degrees or what?

"I believe the two of you have something to say," Mrs. Oates finally invited. "Come stand in front of my desk."

They walked slowly forward.

Theresa blurted, "I didn't want to look. I just accidentally looked the first time. Andy covered his paper. But I looked again. I knew Andy's answers would be right. I might could have finished the problems myself. I just copied his answers." She bowed her head and cried.

Mrs. Oates turned her attention to Andy.

Andy said slowly, "I didn't cover my paper. I allowed Theresa to look." He continued, "I lied to you yesterday by not telling the whole truth. I'm sorry."

Theresa joined in, "I'm sorry too, Mrs. Oates."

Mrs. Oates took the two test papers from her desk, tore them apart, and threw them in the trash can beside her desk.

"These test results are now gone. Only the three of us will know about this incident. The tests will count neither for nor against you. It will not be as easy to deal with your consciences, but they will heal. What you have experienced is a part of growing up, becoming an adult. You compromise yourself each time you cheat or are dishonest. With time you will heal. Do not repeat the process. You will have grown tremendously if you determine never to cheat again."

She walked around her desk to where they were standing and hugged them both at the same time. After a good hug she said, "You're still my children."

She was momentarily unable to continue.

"You may go."

Andy saw tears in her eye. She was as hurt as they were. But he knew they were forgiven.

With heads bowed, they walked slowly from the room.

Mrs. Oates never mentioned the incident again, and, if she treated either of them differently, neither could discern it. She was a good teacher.

Just as Mrs. Oates predicted, the healing process did take some time. For three consecutive days in the late afternoon Andy walked with Doonsie through the fields and by the stream around his home - thinking. He would throw pebbles in the stream and think. He would lean against a tree and think. He would sit on a log and think. He would pat Doonsie and think.

After the first day's walk, he turned to Doonsie and said, "I don't know Doonsie. It hurts. I've let Mrs. Oates down. I'm disappointed in myself." He wrestled with his situation.

Doonsie gave him his sympathetic, understanding look.

He then spent another agonizing night trying to sleep.

After the second day he said, "It hurts a little less Doonsie. Mrs. Oates said it would."

Doonsie never questioned. He never accused.

Andy endured one more fitful night, trying to sleep.

Finally, after the third day's walk, he said to Doonsie, "Doonsie, guilt is not something with which someone else burdens you. Mrs. Oates' questions didn't make me feel guilty. My conscience did." He paused. "Guilt is something that nags you from within because you're not satisfied with yourself, notwithstanding anything anyone else may say for, about, or against you. Mrs. Oates could have told me I acted just fine and I would have still felt guilty." He paused. "Guilt is to the soul as pain is to the body. If I get too close to fire, pain tells me to move my body. If I get too close to wrong, guilt tells me to move my soul." He paused. "Ignore guilt at your peril. Override it to your utter destruction. Deal with its source and be healed."

He determined, as Mrs. Oates had suggested, to never cheat again. That decision made him feel better. And if Mrs. Oates had forgiven him, he would have to find a way to forgive himself.

"Doonsie, as usual, you have been a real friend."

He reached down and patted Doonsie on the head and rubbed his back. They started back home with a bounce in their gaits. Andy was happier. Doonsie was happy if Andy was happy.

ANDY'S BROTHER

The fight was over a girl. Mr. Wade lived in the neighborhood. He sold whiskey for his livelihood. He had a daughter named Maggie. Wayne was a close friend of Andy's family and dated Maggie. Because of an age difference of fifteen years, Mr. Wade didn't want his daughter to date Wayne. He came to Wayne's house to discuss the matter.

The encounter was quick and brutal. Wayne hit Mr. Wade with a hoe and broke his arm. Mr. Wade quickly retreated homeward, arm dangling. When he was well enough, he obtained the services of Lawyer Venters and sued Wayne. Wayne hired Lawyer Summersill and the matter was scheduled for trial. Those were the undisputed bare facts. The disputed facts were to be determined by the jury.

Andy's brother, Dean, had the misfortune to be nearby when the fight occurred. He was caught up in the firestorm. Dean was l4 years old at the time, two years younger than Andy.

The week before the trial was scheduled, Wayne said to Dean, "Let's go for a ride to the store, Dean. We've hoed enough tobacco today. I'll buy you a Pepsi."

On the way back, they stopped under a secluded shade tree to talk and drink their Pepsis.

"You know the trial with Mr. Wade is coming up next week," Wayne said.

"Yes, I do," Dean answered. He began to feel a little uneasy.

"Tell me again. How much of the fight did you see?"

"Well, as I've told you before. I heard Mr. Wade holler. When I came around the corner of the house, Mr. Wade was already running up the road to his house. I really didn't see any of the fight."

"Well, you do know there was a fight?"

"Everybody says there was a fight and I did hear Mr. Wade holler."

"Have you ever seen Mr. Wade with that pistol of his?"

"Yes. I have seen Mr. Wade with his pistol. I have seen him shoot it a couple of times. He uses it to protect himself from the drunks he sells whiskey to."

"That's right. So you know he has a pistol and sells whiskey?"

"Yes."

"Well, he had the pistol the day of the fight. He threatened me with it. To be sure you saw that?" Wayne was insistent.

"No, I told you Wayne. The only thing I saw was Mr. Wade running down the road toward his house."

"Well, if you think about it real hard over the weekend, maybe you can remember the things I just talked with you about. Here. Take this $5.00 bill. I'll talk with you again Monday morning first thing."

Dean didn't take the money so Wayne stuffed the $5.00 bill into Dean's shirt pocket.

Dean said no more as they returned home. Mr. Wade and Wayne were the only persons who actually knew if Mr. Wade had a pistol and threatened Wayne. Dean knew that he did not see any of the fight. The matter weighed heavily on his mind for two days.

"You look kind of down, Dean," Andy said.

"Wayne wants me to testify at the trial next week about some things I didn't see. He wants me to say I saw Mr. Wade with a pistol. Gave me $5.00."

"Tried to bribe you, huh?"

"That's exactly what it is."

"You could just give the $5.00 back to him and insist you didn't see anything."

"Everybody will be mad at me. The whole family wants Wayne to win at the trial. Everyone thinks Mr. Wade's just a bootlegger, you know."

"I see what you mean. Lot of pressure on you. I still think you've got to give the $5.00 back. Want me to do it for you?"

"No, I'll do it myself. Everybody will still be mad at me for not helping Wayne. I just have to think about it."

In addition to having a sensitive conscience, Dean was also impulsive. He finally extracted himself from his dilemma by running away. No one knew at the time, but he went to Rocky Mount and found a job as a gas station attendant.

On one of his walks with Doonsie, Andy discussed the matter. "You know, Doonsie, I'm not worried about Dean too much. He can take care of himself. He does take things kind of hard, might react too hastily, but I think he'll be alright. Probably be back in a few days, after the trial is over."

They walked along the river.

"This lying business, though - I don't know. As a practical matter, it can get you a few years in jail for perjury."

They walked along the river.

"Then there's another side of lying. If Mr. Wade had a pistol, it would seem harmless enough for Dean to say he saw it - just a little white lie to help out the truth. That's probably what Wayne is thinking. But wouldn't something suffer? Just take a look at the turmoil Dean is suffering. Wrecks the conscience, I'd say. And Dean was just asked to lie. He hasn't even told a lie yet."

They walked along the river.

"You know, Doonsie, people can lie to themselves. Wayne has probably convinced, or is trying to convince, himself that lying is the best thing to do. But once you start down that road, who knows where it will end?"

They walked along the river.

"Anyway. The truth is the truth and a lie won't change it. Truth will take care of itself. The liar needs to beware. He may start believing his own lies."

As usual, Doonsie was the good listener. The only reward he wanted was a good pat and kind words. Andy obliged.

Without an important witness, Wayne and Mr. Wade settled out of court, agreeing to a consent judgment whereby Wayne would pay Mr. Wade $l,800.00.

Dean stayed gone for four weeks until he was sure the trial was over. He never explained to anyone his reasons for running away. If anyone knew about the $5.00 payment he did not talk of it openly. Wayne remained a friend of the family. He gave the settlement amount in cash to Andy for delivery to the Onslow County Clerk of Superior Court.

When Dean returned he brought his impulsive nature with him. He would wrestle with that problem all of his life. But lying was not his beast.

THE FIGHT

Gong went the bell,
For heavyweights, tall,
A fight for the soul,
And winner takes all.

Truth in this corner,
With appearance so drab,
A future that's bright,
But too distant to grab.

A lie in this corner,
An attractive hulk,
His promise is now,
Trust in my bulk.

With lunacy a veil,
And blind by deceit,
The crowd couldn't see,
The worms eating his feet.

The lie led with lefts,
Followed by rights,
But Truth stood undaunted,
Not a blemish in sight.

But Truth soon discovered,
The lie hard to pen,
He danced and moved,
A sliding scale, his friend.

Finally discouraged,
By a chorus of boos,
Truth crashed to the canvas,
He allowed them to choose.

No mourning the vanquished,
But the crowd left behind,
They preferred the glitter,
Not the genuine find.

No mourning the vanquished,
The lie has his time,
But there'll be a rematch,
The count reached just nine.

THE LAST SUMMER

Andy graduated from high school in June. He had been thinking for some time about his future. Some classmates would go off to college. He could not afford college. Some classmates found jobs immediately. Andy didn't. He had not even tried. Finishing school had been his priority. He had been single-minded about that effort. What to do now? He approached that decision just as all others. When he had time, he pondered.

He decided to help his grandpa and Uncle Clyde, Alvin's brother, farm that summer and harvest the crops in the fall. That would give him time to consider all of his options - and ponder. He knew there were some decisions to be made, namely, what to do with the rest of his life. He had thought about it before, but his thinking now became more focused. He was, as usual, in no hurry.

He would talk with Doonsie throughout the summer about his situation.

"You know, Doonsie, I have some important decisions to make. Come this fall, I'm not going to be around here as much as I'm used to. Got to go off to some job. Make a living. Make my mark in the world. All of that stuff, you know."

Doonsie paid close attention.

"Got any suggestions?"

Doonsie knew he was being called upon and lowered his head when he had no response.

Andy patted him on the head to let him know no response was expected.

Doonsie wagged his tail. They had been friends for a long time now.

"Well, you're still not much of a conversationalist - but a mighty good listener," Andy smiled. "That helps more than you can know."

Doonsie wagged his tail again.

"How about a doctor, a lawyer, an Indian chief?" Andy paused. "If you think about it, Doonsie, it really doesn't matter. Doctors have their problems. Lawyers have their problems. I don't know much about being an Indian Chief, but I'll wager a hefty sum it's the same with them."

Doonsie wagged his tail again when he heard his name called.

Andy concluded, "As long as it's honest, and, like grandpa says, you pay your own way, I guess it doesn't much matter how you get through this life. We're all laid to rest in the end. As Mr. Stevens likes to say, 'You don't see a U-haul trailer behind a hearse'." Andy paused for some time. "I'll find me a respectable job and make a respectable living."

Andy and Doonsie played tug-of-war all the way back home. Tug-of-war was Doonsie's version of fetch. He would fetch any stick Andy would throw, but he never wanted to give up the stick. A tug-of-war resulted. Andy would playfully wrestle away the stick after a few half-hearted growls from Doonsie. They then repeated the process.

They took their time. There was no need to hurry. Tomorrow would arrive on time.

Andy swam in Jack Island during the dinner break from putting in tobacco. He swam in Jack Island on weekends. He went fishing by himself. He went fishing with Alvin. He went to Richlands on weekends for a movie. He joined in the conversations with everyone at Laney's barbershop and the general store.

He talked with David about their plans as they sat on the banks of Jack Island after a swim.

"David, have you thought about what you're going to do when we're through with the tobacco crops?"

"Yep, I think I might get a job with the power company. I'm already doing that on weekends now."

"I didn't know that. When did you start working on weekends?"

"About three weeks back. The company says I can go full time in the fall. How about you?"

"Still don't know. Haven't made up my mind."

"I'm not surprised. You never were one to hurry."

They smiled. They relaxed in the calm around Jack Island.

David broke the silence. "The water is getting low again. Hardly enough to swim in. We need some rain."

"Still not as bad as three years ago. That was a drought to remember," Andy answered.

"Yeah, it will be talked about for a long time."

They enjoyed the quiet.

David again broke the silence. "We ought to ride over to the state park in Goldsboro tomorrow. More water to swim in. The Neuse River is pretty big there."

"Sounds good to me. But I didn't know there was a place to swim there."

"Oh, yes, and there's a floating platform in the middle of the river for diving."

"We'll try it," Andy agreed.

They did visit the state park. There was plenty of water just as David had said. Andy was impressed with the view from the cliffs and the meadow. He decided he would return when he had more time to explore.

The summer passed all too quickly. Students began to board school buses in late August. Andy watched the children. He took note that he was passing a milestone in his life.

"Doonsie, don't you wonder why I'm not getting on the bus?"

He paused.

"Well, I'm not a kid any more."

He watched the school bus disappear around a corner.

"And don't look so superior; you're no pup either."

For the first time in his life, Andy lamented the passing of time. To his dismay, his world was changing.

Harvest Ends

Tobacco harvesting ran into September that year. On the last harvest day Andy helped grandpa clean up around the barn after grandma had gone to the house to prepare supper. All other helpers had gone home. They started the wood fire in the furnace for curing the tobacco and sat and watched as the temperature in the barn began to rise. They sat close to the fire since there was a late evening September chill in the air. Grandpa was the only farmer in the neighborhood still using wood. Most had converted to oil or gas.

Grandpa didn't like change either.

Cricket chirps were subdued because of the cool temperature. Frogs had hushed altogether. The tobacco stalks, now minus all their leaves, suggested a spent summer. A few leaves on the trees were beginning to turn orange or brown. The sunset was a lowery red.

The season was changing.

"Did you ever think of curing with oil or gas, grandpa?" Andy began.

"Yeah, I thought about it. Decided against it."

"Why?"

"Well, I was born in the last century. I grew up in the first part of this century. I'm essentially a l9th century man in a 20th century world. I'm comfortable curing with wood. Being comfortable with your surroundings gives you time to consider more important things. No need to change just for change's sake. Oh, if I stayed around long enough, I'd probably finally change. Just no need to change at my age."

"Most farmers made the change l5 to 20 years ago."

"I know, Andy, I know. I'm in no hurry. Where are we going in such a hurry anyway?"

"Don't we have to stay up with this modern world?"

"Sometimes you do. But if you rush to stay up, it will cost you. If it does pull you along, you must still make time for the important things."

"You know, grandpa, I believe the way I do about a lot of things because of what you have said to me over the years."

"I consider that a mighty fine compliment, Andy."

Grandma called out from the house, "Supper time." Grandma still used a cook stove heated with wood. As far as Andy was concerned, that was proof enough that all change was not good. Nobody could cook a better meal on those electric stoves.

They ate and returned to the barn.

Andy and grandpa made pillows of flour sacks and fixed a 'bed' on two of the tobacco trucks where they would spend the night. Doonsie lay on the ground by Andy's tobacco-truck 'bed'. Grandpa would occasionally add wood to the fire, slowly raising the temperature in the barn.

"What are the important things, grandpa?"

"How's that, Andy?"

"You know, a while ago you said that being comfortable with your surroundings gave you time to consider more important things."

"Oh, yes. Well, your surroundings are just your existence. Food, clothes, shelter, things like that. Now I'm not saying they are not important. You got to work for your living. But can you pass through this world and maintain your identity? Can you have more effect on the world for good than the world has on you for bad? Can you treat your fellow-man fairly and kindly though he may not treat you that way? Can you contribute and not just take? Are you oil for the world's machinery or are you a loose wrench in its cogs? What preparations do you make to meet God?"

Grandpa stopped talking.

The sun had disappeared and the stars were making their appearance. The fire, the only light except the stars and fireflies, was warm in the cool of the night. Grandpa had said a lot. They lay on their tobacco-truck 'beds'. They were quiet, each with his own thoughts - ruminating. They rested, mind as well as body.

Andy finally asked, "Does God ever talk to us, grandpa?"

"We shout; God whispers. I'm afraid we most often don't hear Him because of the sound of our own voices."

Grandpa turned over on his tobacco-truck 'bed'.

"God's method of conversation is more often experience, not words. He may not even speak English."

Andy would have to think about that.

A little later Andy turned to practical matters and said, "You know, grandpa, I have to find me a job pretty soon."

"I'm not worried about you, Andy. I have watched you grow up. You're solid. You'll do alright."

"It's a big world, grandpa."

"Just take one bite at a time. You can chew it up." Grandpa took one more chance to teach. "Remember, Andy, success may just be waving 'Hello' to more people than wave to you as you walk down the street."

They cured tobacco and slept. It was a sound sleep, made possible only by the surrounding peace, tired bodies, and clear consciences.

As it happened, Andy didn't need to look for a job. He was drafted. The notice came in October. He was to report to the recruiting office in New Bern on the second Monday in January of the coming year. That was three months away. Andy could help grandpa gather his corn. The remaining time would be used to say goodbye to friends and places.

David and Andy went squirrel hunting one last time. They spent the night at David's house and set the alarm clock so that they could be in the woods by sunrise. A cold front had moved through the day before. The accompanying rain had left the leaves wet so that they were able to walk through the woods without much sound. The temperature had fallen 40 degrees from that of two days before. Frost covered the fields around the woods. They quietly entered the woods and took their places to wait for squirrels to come out of hiding. In muffled tones they talked.

"You know, Andy, fate is a strange thing. Here I am going to work for the electric company. I'm going to get married next spring. You ain't even thought about getting married and you're going off to the army in January. Who decides such things? Is it our destiny? Is it our fate?"

"I don't know if it's only fate, David. We do have something to say about what happens to us."

"Oh, yeah. Just don't report next January and see what happens."

"Well, I admit some things are decided for us. But I kind of believe that we work with fate, if you will, and whatever happens is what we decide together."

"What if you go off to India there and get killed? You know, they are beginning to do some real hard fighting over there."

"It's Vietnam. That's where they are fighting. And I certainly hope that doesn't happen. If it does, you can have my shotgun." Andy smiled.

"Don't be laughing about a thing like that. You know I'd miss you. I know I'm a little rough around the edges, but you have been my best friend all these years."

Andy realized that David was making his best effort to say goodbye. "I'll be careful, David. You look after yourself around here while I'm gone."

They finished their hunting without saying much.

"There's one," David said. "It's your turn to shoot. Go ahead."

"Your shot," Andy said as they took turns.

They bagged five squirrels and took them to David's house for dressing. David's mother would cook them for supper. They rode around the neighborhood before supper. They rode around *Toot and Tell It*, the school house, and downtown Richlands.

Andy suggested that they ride over to the state park in Goldsboro.

"Ain't nothing much there this time of year. The beach is closed."

"We'll have the place all to ourselves."

"Okay with me. It'll give us some place to go. Won't take us over an hour there and back. Supper will be ready."

David was right. The beach was closed. The place appeared abandoned. Park rangers were scarce. Andy and David walked to the edge of the cliffs and watched the river below wind its way to the Atlantic Ocean. Andy noted that azaleas were plentiful but not in bloom. He thought that it would be a beautiful place to visit in the spring.

They meandered back to Onslow County and returned to David's house. They ate stewed squirrels and rice for supper.

Everyone waved as Andy drove away.

All Aboard

Andy's mom had been dreading the departure day. Tears were increasingly hard to hold back. Sometimes she failed.

"Mom," Andy said, "I think I'll spend tonight down by the river with Alvin. I'll come back first thing in the morning. I think Alvin will take me to New Bern."

Bess's eyes moistened as she watched Andy leave.

After eating supper and washing the supper dishes with sand, Andy and Alvin took their usual seats around the fire. The dogs settled down too.

"Are you going to take me to New Bern tomorrow, Alvin?"

"Sure thing, if you want me to."

"I'd appreciate it. I had rather say goodbye to the family at the house. Won't have to be so much fussing at the recruiting office."

They relaxed.

"You know, I'll probably end up in Vietnam. That's where most of the draftees end up."

"Where?"

"Vietnam. Southeast Asia. They been fighting over there for a while now."

"I've read a little about it. Don't know what we're fighting about though."

They rested.

"Tell me about war, Alvin."

"It's bad."

"You've never told me about your injuries. Do you want to talk about it?"

"War is bad, Andy. War is bad."

Even though Alvin's repeated response was not as tart as usual, Andy knew Alvin meant to forget the subject and that no other response was forthcoming. Andy moved on.

"They told me to bring only a toothbrush and a shaving kit, Alvin. Not even a change of clothes. Can you believe that?" Andy pulled his transistor radio from his jacket pocket and offered it to Alvin. "I'm not going to be needing this. Would you like to have it?"

Alvin hesitated. The radio in his pickup had been inoperable for some time now. He had no television or radio. "You know I like my solitude, Andy. It won't bust in on me will it?"

"You can have it and just not play it unless you want to."

"You can leave it if you want to. I might play it sometime."

"Do you want to hear it now?"

"Okay."

Andy tuned the radio to an easy-listening station located in Greenville. They advertised "No rock none of the time." He figured that station's style would more suit Alvin than the rock and roll played on most stations. He turned the volume up just a little, and they listened. The usual advertisements were broadcast and then a series of Irish ballads was played. The singers reminisced about their lost or frustrated loves. Andy had almost fallen asleep listening.

"You know, Andy. I had a girl one time."

Andy was startled, first, because Alvin had breached the quiet and, second, because of the tone of Alvin's voice. His voice was wavering. He also had never heard Alvin talk about his past before.

Andy managed to ask, "When?"

"Before the war. Her name was Kathleen."

Alvin's voice faded so that Andy could not understand the name.

"What was her name?"

"Kathleen."

"What happened to her?"

Alvin started to speak on three occasions but could not without choking up. "She .... I ....We......." He finally gave up.

Andy asked no more. He turned off the radio and they turned in for the night's sleep without another word. As Andy drifted off to sleep, he thought of Alvin's lost love and the kind of person she might have been. He also thought of a girl he had yet to know.

UNREQUITED LOVE

Longing, endured,
For the present a gentle aching,
Each changing tide expectation-filled,
Makes worthwhile the waiting,
And a simple touch divine.

Tears, shed,
For joy or sorrow,
Till the soul in winter,
Tenderness prevailing,
With love blossoming in spring.

Moments, treasured,
Preserve the heart tender,
Though hours, labored,
Would like a brine,
Render it acrid.

Secrets, shared,
And eternally retained,
To all the world a mystery,
The tether broken,
Become an everlasting bond.

Promises, sweet,
Yet fulfilled or broken,
Anticipation quickening,
Excite the heart presently,
Though tomorrow may bring either.

Love, unrequited,
Because of wayward stars only,
Still warms the heart daily,
And hopes that the heavens will,
With splendid harmony, amend.

Andy had no trouble with basic training. He was used to saying "Yes, sir" and "No, sir" which, with little effort, became "Yes, Drill Sergeant" and "No, Drill Sergeant". The training made sense to him. If you were going off to war, you needed to be prepared. He subsequently felt that the war would be easy after enduring sixteen weeks of basic training.

He did meet Robert D. Riddle. Riddle, like Andy, was from North Carolina as in Raleigh.

"I'm Riddle," Robert said as they waited in line for their issue of uniforms.

"I'm Andrew Goodday," Andy said forgetting that last names were used in the service.

"Where you from, Goodday?"

"Richlands, North Carolina."

"You're kidding. I'm from North Carolina too. Raleigh."

They shook hands.

"No place in the world like good ole North Carolina," Riddle said.

"You can say that again. I'd give a pretty penny to be there right now."

"And me with you, good buddy," Riddle pined.

They became best friends. They ate chow together. They went on their first weekend liberty together after the eighth week of training. They played chess together on weekends. They swam together at the camp pool. Riddle was a good diver. They finished basic training together.

They were both chosen for further training in communications equipment repair. The school was to last sixteen additional weeks after basic training. They couldn't believe it. This war, at least for the present, was not going to be so bad after all.

Their friendship continued to grow. The schooling was the best of times. Bob gave Andy the address of a girl named Judi in Raleigh. They would remain pen pals throughout Andy's service. Andy gave Theresa's address to Bob. They corresponded and were to meet immediately after Bob's discharge.

Andy and Bob were the top two students in the class. They competed against each other ferociously. But they helped each other study at night. Andy would obtain the top grade one week. Bob would obtain the top grade the next. The other was always second. Each enjoyed seeing the other succeed.

But Vietnam loomed.

Immediately after completing their equipment repair schooling they were attached to a supply depot just north of Saigon. The duty for the most part was relatively safe.

Andy did make one more friend when he arrived. As Andy was accustomed to doing, he was walking around the compound one night after everyone had turned in. The little dog, about half the size of Doonsie, was raiding the garbage cans behind the mess hall. When he saw Andy, he dashed off to a safe distance. Andy had seen him before, but Andy nor anyone had been able to get close to the little critter.

"What you up to, little buddy?" Andy asked softly.

The dog's ears perked up, but he kept his distance.

"Wouldn't you like to be friends?"

The dog paced back and forth.

"You know, I have a dog back home. He's a whole lot healthier than you though."

The dog would not be coaxed and kept his distance.

The next night Andy had saved part of his supper and brought it with him. He sat down close to the garbage cans and waited. The dog finally made his appearance.

"Well, this must be your routine. I figured as much. Not much pickin's around here is there? Would you like this?" Andy tossed the supper he had brought about half the distance between himself and the dog. The dog backed away. Andy had to back away before the dog slowly approached the supper and ate. When Andy tried to get close, he retreated.

On the third night Andy sat down close to the cans. When the dog made his appearance, he tossed the supper just a short distance from himself and waited.

"If you want supper, you'll have to come closer."

The dog finally came close enough to eat. Still no contact.

On the fourth night Andy tossed the food very close and waited. The dog was less reluctant and came forward to eat. After finishing, he sat down.

"You know, that same moon up there will be shining on North Carolina in just a few hours. I sure wish it was shining on me standing in North Carolina. Only ten more moons to go and I'll be going home. What do you think about that?"

The dog relaxed.

"I have one more piece of meat. But you're going to have to take it from my hand." Andy held the meat toward the dog.

The dog slowly moved forward and took the meat from Andy's hand.

"Well, that wasn't so bad, was it?"

The next night Andy fed him from his hand and patted him on his head. As Andy talked, the dog sat down by Andy and listened.

"Well, you're no Doonsie, but I reckon you'll do. I think I'll call you Raider. How's that?"

Raider would finally rush to Andy with tail waggling. They would 'talk' until Andy's return home to North Carolina. Andy would feed Raider. Raider would comfort Andy when times got tough.

After nine months, there had been little more than a few sporadic mortar rounds to break the monotony of supplying and repairing communications equipment and waiting for the one-year tour of duty to expire. Andy and Bob had helped return some small arms fire at the perimeter of the base. Other than that, they had not seen much of 'Charlie'. 'Charlie' was the North Vietnamese soldier. But all soldiers, supply company included, were expected to be ready to fight.

The platoon sergeant yelled out. "Riddle. Goodday. Be ready first thing in the morning, 0600. You're with the unit delivering supplies to Delta sector tomorrow. It's about a thirty mile trip. May stay overnight. Full battle gear."

"Sarge, we haven't been off the depot since we got here," Riddle complained.

"I know that. We're a little short-handed. Your job will be to drive. But be ready for anything."

Bob and Andy looked at each other. Their heart rates increased. Both knew that the fighting frequency had accelerated around Saigon. They had seen some body bags.

"Looks like we're going to get a little closer to this war, Andy."

"I reckon so. We had better start packing."

At 0600, the convoy began assembling. There were ten trucks. Three were loaded with marine grunts. The rest, loaded with supplies, had army supply-company drivers. A jeep carried a mounted 50-caliber machine gun and the company lieutenant.

The road became more narrow as they traveled. It was finally little more than a cart path. About 25 miles into the trip, the war got real close. At first it was just five mortar shells exploding along the road. No hits.

"Get out of those trucks. Take cover," the sergeant yelled.

Andy and Bob grabbed their M-l6's and jumped into a ditch beside the road. The muddy water was no impediment. They ducked their heads as the mortar explosions increased in number.

AK-47 fire began coming from the left. The marines engaged 'Charlie' and seemed to drive him back. AK-47 fire began coming from the right. The marines retreated to a more secure position near the trucks and returned the fire to the right.

Mortar rounds continued to increase in number and began finding their marks. Two trucks exploded.

"Where are they coming from? This is supposed to be a clean sector," the sergeant yelled.

AK-47 fire began coming from the rear.

"Look out. More of them behind us," the sergeant yelled. "We're surrounded."

The lieutenant ordered, "See if we can make that small hill over yonder and secure a position. Get moving."

They would have to fight their way through 'Charlie' to get to the hill. The lieutenant also called in artillery support and big l6-inch shells began falling on 'Charlie's' position on the other side of the road.

And they fought.

'Charlie' was no more than 75 feet away when Andy made his first hit. 'Charlie' crumpled to the ground. As Andy ran past, he shot him four more times to make certain he was dead.

A big shell exploded close to Andy. The concussion knocked Andy into an old shell crater. When he recovered his senses, he saw a 'Charlie' lying just five feet from him. 'Charlie's' right arm was missing from just below the shoulder. The stump was bleeding profusely. There was an open wound in his chest and it was covered in blood. Andy checked himself. Except for a piercing headache, he discovered no wounds.

Since Andy had reached the bottom of the hill, he waited as the rest of the company assembled around the hill. He watched as helicopter gun ships annihilated 'Charlie's' position with rockets and machine-gun fire. He thought that nothing could be alive down there. Hell could hardly be worse.

As he was watching, he heard something stir behind him. He turned to see 'Charlie' reaching for his AK-47 with his left hand. He was so disabled he could not manage. He was still trying. Andy raised his M-l6 and pointed it at 'Charlie'. They looked at each other. 'Charlie' waited stoically for his execution. Andy could not do it. He reached toward 'Charlie'. 'Charlie' turned his face away expecting to die. Andy picked up his AK-47 and tossed it away.

The carnage below finally stopped. The helicopters disappeared into the distance. If anything was left of 'Charlie', he had retreated into the jungle. It was over as quickly as it had started. It was quiet, not a sound.

The lieutenant, about 200 feet from Andy, finally stood and ordered the men to assemble around him.

Andy looked again at 'Charlie'. He leaned over and took a cloth from 'Charlie's' waist and tied it around the stump of his severed arm. He gathered 'Charlie's' shirt into a ball and stuck it in the open wound in the right side of his chest and pressed 'Charlie's' left hand on the gathered shirt. He stood and bowed to 'Charlie'. 'Charlie' bowed his head as best he could. Andy then closed ranks around the lieutenant.

Andy watched anxiously as the soldiers and marines began to gather around the lieutenant. He wanted desperately to see Bob. Bob did not appear.

The troop began to make its way back down the hill to the trucks. One American soldier saw the 'Charlie' Andy had helped and shot him with a burst from his M-I6. Andy turned his head.

Andy checked each American body as he went. Bob had not made it out of the ditch beside the road. He lay face down in the mud. Andy retrieved his body and carried it to the edge of the ditch. He sat down and cradled Bob in his arms. When the MediVac helicopters arrived, corpsmen had to pry Andy's arms from around Bob.

Andy watched as they carried his best friend away.

After the supply delivery was complete, Andy returned to his hut and sat down. Riddle's bunk and foot locker were directly beside his. He remembered Riddle. He could not hold back the tears which flowed down his cheeks. He did not try.

"I'm sorry about your friend," the sergeant said as he interrupted Andy's meditation. "It was not supposed to be this way. It was supposed to be a safe assignment. You just don't know about this crazy war."

He waited for Andy to respond. Andy did not.

"We've got to inventory and pack Riddle's things. I'll help you."

"Let me do it, Sarge."

The sergeant shook his head and asked, "You going to be all right, Goodday?"

Andy nodded his head. "I'll have them ready in the morning."

Andy stored his own equipment which he had packed for the trip and then spent the evening packing Riddle's belongings. Letters. Pictures. Clothes. A Bible. Andy opened the Bible where the marker was located. Bob had underlined Revelation 2l:4. "And God shall wipe away all tears from their eyes; and there shall be no more death, neither sorrow, nor crying, neither shall there be any more pain: for the former things are passed away." He felt comforted.

He piled everything into one neat stack and watched the next morning as it was carried away for shipment to Raleigh, North Carolina.

Andy wrote letters.

Dear Judi,

I regret to inform you that Bob was killed in action. We will remember him.

You have been a good pen pal. I hope we will be able to talk more when I get back home.

Your Pen Pal,

Andy

Dear Mr. and Mrs. Riddle,

Your son was my best friend. A man could not have a better friend. We were alike in many ways.

If you like, I will visit you when I return home. We will remember Bob together.

Yours truly,

Andy Goodday

Dear Mom and Dad,

I lost my best friend. I feel like I have lost part of me. It will be hard to recover. Time will help.

Your son,

Andy

Dear Theresa,

I'm sorry you never got to meet Bob. You would have liked him.

Andy

Alvin,

I think I now better understand why you do not like to talk about war. It is bad. The dead are no more. The living suffer.

There was a time in a shell crater when I came face to face with 'Charlie'. If he and I had been the only participants, the war would have been over. I saw another human being. I could not kill him. Who made us fight? The war began in someone's heart somewhere and spread to mine and Charlie's.

Andy

Andy received more bad news when his mom's reply came.

Dearest Andy,

I'm sorry to have to tell you all of this bad news at one time, but I didn't want you to come home expecting to see someone who's not going to be here. Your grandpa and Alvin are dead.

Your grandpa had a stroke. He lingered for two weeks and finally died.

No one knows exactly how Alvin died. He had been dead for some time when they found him. The body was decomposed. Cause of death was unknown. Since it was an unattended death there was an investigation. They found an aspirin bottle half empty and a purchase receipt dated for about the time they think he died. It could have been accidental. No one knows. He had a will and left all of his earthly belongings to you.

That little dog you were so fond of died too. He just sort of wasted away after you left. He didn't want anything to do with anybody. He was quite old.

It has all happened so suddenly. I didn't know how to handle telling you. Our prayers are with you. Please come home soon.

With all our love,

Mom and Dad

Andy laid the letter on his bunk and hung his head. He finally took a walk.

He talked with Raider.

"Raider, this world can be tough, little buddy. But I guess you know that. In the last three months I have lost three people who were very precious to me. I have lost one little dog who was my best friend for a long time". Andy could say no more. He retreated inward with his thoughts.

After a while he said, "Raider, we just have to keep searching for the showers."

He was not sorry to leave Vietnam.

WAR

The lines are drawn,
The forces that be,
Armed to the teeth;
It's honor you see.

The battle is raging,
With good in retreat;
Evil pressed on;
Common sense in defeat.

The fighting continues,
Till sight is lost,
Blinded by hate,
Never counting the cost.

The carnage of nightmares,
Truth falls to the left,
No prisoners be taken,
It's worthy of death.

The outcome in doubt,
Till I surrendered my will,
For the battleground's my bosom,
Elusive victory my seal.

HOMECOMING

The bus stopped at Haw Branch Road. Alvin's place, grandpa's place, and Jack Island were just a short distance away. Andy disembarked with discharge orders in hand. He had answered his country's call. He stretched and took a deep breath as the driver retrieved his baggage. The smell was wonderful. No place on earth smelled like Haw Branch to Andy. Or was it just that his senses were sharper? Either way, he was home.

The bus driver deposited his baggage beside Andy, snapped to attention, and gave a smart salute. "I appreciate your service, soldier. Thank you."

Andy, somewhat surprised, returned the salute without a word.

The driver then patted Andy on the shoulder, got on the bus, and drove away. Andy was alone.

He sat down on his baggage and enjoyed the peace and quiet of a country road. He tried to synchronize his senses with the surroundings. His service time and Vietnam had dictated a pace which was alien to Andy. He knew he had changed. He did not realize how much he had changed until just now. It would take a long time he thought, if ever, to repatriate himself. Some things could not be recovered. Alvin was dead. Grandpa was dead. Doonsie was dead.

He finally placed his baggage in the bushes by the road. He would return and retrieve it later. He then began his walk down Haw Branch Road. He hoped it would lead to yesterday. He knew better, but he would try.

If he had any doubts that yesterday was gone, they disappeared when he reached the river. He hardly recognized the place. The cart path to Alvin's place was still there, but the river resembled a big ditch. The bridge had been removed, and the waters were accommodated by a concrete culvert. The river had been cleaned of vines, decaying logs, and other debris. Trees along the river had been cut and removed. The channel had been widened. He walked along the river and finally arrived at Jack Island. It was more accurate to say that he arrived at the spot where Jack Island had once been located. The rock causing the formation of Jack Island had been removed. The water was only ankle deep. He searched intensely, but he was not sure of the location where he had learned to swim. He was not sure of the spot where grandpa had built his many diving boards. The log he sat upon for his talks with Doonsie was gone. He returned to the road and sat down on a corner of the concrete culvert and tried to remember.

Andy was aroused from his reflections by the sound of an approaching vehicle. It was Mr. Stevens.

"Is that you, Andy?" Mr. Stevens asked as he pulled along side Andy and got out of his pickup truck.

"Hey Mr. Stevens. Yes, it's me." Andy tossed into the river a stick he had been using to fiddle in the sand. He reluctantly left his reflections behind to join changing reality.

"What in the world did they do to the river?" Andy asked.

"All in the name of flood control, son. Ruined it, didn't they?"

"I mean they did. It's hardly deep enough to get your feet wet."

"It's a shame," Mr. Stevens said, joining Andy's reflective mood. "But tell me about yourself. How have you been? Are you home for good?"

"Yep. I'm home for good. Got my discharge orders right here in my pocket," Andy said while patting his shirt.

"Well. I'm mighty glad to have you back, son."

They shook hands.

"I'm glad to be back, Mr. Stevens."

"What you doing down here by yourself?"

"I just got off the bus on the main road. I'm headed home."

"Want a ride?"

"I'll ride with you to your house and then walk the rest of the way. I want to just sort of take my time."

"I think I know what you mean."

Mr. Stevens drove slowly, giving Andy time to observe. They talked of small things. Andy got out at Mr. Stevens' driveway and continued his walk home.

Hugging

The family meeting was all hugging with a few tears mixed in.

Mom couldn't wait to serve supper. "You look thin, Andy. Did they feed you well?"

"They fed me pretty good, Mom. It was just not as good as yours though."

After supper Andy's dad and Andy returned to the main road to retrieve his baggage. They talked of some fishing and just taking things easy.

Andy did take things easy. He would rise early and sit on the porch. This went on for two days. Andy's mother began to worry some.

"You going to be all right, Andy?"

"Yes, Mom. I'm all right. I'm just trying to make some sense out of things."

"That's pretty hard sometimes. Things can get pretty complicated."

"Where do I go from here, Mom?" He pondered. "The world is not as young and as full of promise as it once was. I feel old right this minute."

"You've been through a lot. Times are always changing. Just take things easy, Andy You'll figure it out."

She reached over and kissed Andy on his cheek.

"I'm just so glad to have you home."

Visiting David

Late in the third day he decided to visit David. David would be home from his job with the power company by this time. He was home and he was mowing his yard. He cut the mower off as Andy came into the yard.

"Andy? Where in the world did you come from?" They shook hands.

"I got home three days ago. I'm just now trying to get around to see everyone."

"I knew you were coming home, but I didn't know exactly when. It's good to see you."

"It's good to be back." Andy paused and looked around. "So this is where you're staying? You've got it looking good."

"Yeah, we're renting right now. Hope to start building our own home in a couple of years."

They had hardly started their conversation when a toddler came running from the house and wrapped his arms around David's leg.

"This is David, Junior. Say hello to Mr. Goodday, Junior."

"Hello," the little fellow finally said with some coaxing.

Andy played with Junior trying to get him to repeat his name but with little success. He turned to David again. "Well, you're all grown up and married."

"Yeah. Got one more inside the house. Just two months old. His name's Johnny. They're both a handful."

"I can imagine. Or maybe I can't. I don't even want to think of kids right now."

"They can tie you down. No more *Toot and Tell It*. No more weekends with nothing but loafing. Seems like I've been with the power company forever." David seemed wistful as he remembered the carefree days with Andy.

His thoughts were interrupted by his wife. "David, supper in 30 minutes. You need to finish that yard before dark."

"Okay. Okay. Andy's here. I'm just saying hello."

"Oh. I didn't know who that was. Ask him if he wants to stay for supper."

David turned to Andy.

"No, none for me. I just stopped by to say hello. I didn't plan to stay long." Andy felt that he was an extra in the scene.

"Stay if you'd like. We'd love to have you," David said as he started his mower.

"I'll come another time. We'll do some heavy talking."

"That sounds good. Come by any time."

Andy waved and walked away. He knew that any time really meant no time in particular and that it was probably not going to happen. The childhood David he had known was no more.

Visiting Raleigh

On the fourth day home Andy asked, "Mom, will it be alright to use your car? I want to see Bob's parents and visit Bob's grave in Raleigh."

"Certainly. How long you going to be gone?"

"Probably till tomorrow. I have called Judi, you know, my pen pal. We are going to eat supper together."

"Oh, you have a date."

"Sort of. We're just going to get together for some conversation."

"Sounds like a date to me."

"We'll see."

The Riddles

Mr. and Mrs. Riddle were as nice as Andy thought they would be. They invited him right into their home.

"Come on in," Mrs. Riddle said. "We're so glad to have you."

Mr. Riddle joined in making him feel welcomed. "Come on in, son. The missus is right. We're glad to have you."

Andy sat down in their living room.

"I expect you would like something to drink after your trip? We have tea or a soft drink."

"Tea will be fine."

As Mrs. Riddle served tea, Andy noticed pictures of Bob scattered throughout the room.

"He was our only child," Mrs. Riddle said as she gathered the pictures and presented them to Andy. "This is a picture of his high school diving team. This is his graduation picture. He was about eight years old in this one. Here he was riding his new bike for the first time." She could not continue. She left the remaining pictures for Andy to look at without further explanation.

Andy looked at all the pictures and laid them beside Mrs. Riddle. "He was my best friend, Mrs. Riddle."

Andy waited for Mrs. Riddle to wipe away her tears.

"Do you want to know how he died?"

Mr. and Mrs. Riddle looked at each other. Mr. Riddle finally said, "They told us he was shot."

"Yes, we were ambushed. We returned fire, but we were surrounded. We all tried to secure a position away from our convoy. Before we could, Bob was hit by rifle fire from the jungle. He fought well."

Everyone was quiet.

"I would like to visit his grave," Andy said.

"It's just a short distance from here."

Mr. Riddle gave directions. Mrs. Riddle hugged Andy. They waved goodbye.

Bob's Grave

Bob's headstone read "Robert D. Riddle. Corporal. U.S. Army. Vietnam. Born April 4, 1947. Died April 20, 1968."

"It does not do you justice. -------- You were much more than that. -------- They should have put that you were my friend, Mr. and Mrs. Riddle's son. ------- They should have put that you rode bicycles. -------- It just seems too brief."

Andy sat down on an adjoining footstone.

"I read the Bible section you had underlined. ------- I hope you have found your place where there are no more tears. ------- I look for such a place. ------- I hope to meet you there."

Andy watched the sun fall below the horizon.

He said softly just before leaving, "Robert D. Riddle, I will remember you."

Judi

Judi was as pretty as her picture. She had a cute little nose. They decided on pizza for supper.

She was about to enter her third year of college. She wanted a home. She wanted a family. Her plans for the future seemed to stretch on indefinitely. She was excited and hurriedly shared it all with Andy.

She turned her attentions to Andy. "How about you, Andy?"

"Well, right now..." Andy had only begun to think about her first question before she had showered him with two more.

"What are your plans? Do you have job prospects?"

"Well, not really. I'm not in any....."

She interrupted. "How about college? Do you think you might go?"

"Maybe. But it takes a lot of...."

"You ought to, you know. You're never going to get any place in this world without college."

"I agree it will help. I just haven't made up my mind."

"Oh," Judi said as her voice faded with obvious disappointment.

Andy was glad when the pizza was finally served. Maybe that would slow the pace of the conversation. He kept thinking that they were like two ships passing in the night, each unaware of the other. Or maybe they were like two ships headed in the same direction, and Judi had lapped him. Either way, the communications were garbled. Andy suspected that Judi had interpreted his pace as lack of desire and ambition. He was not sure. They both knew before the pizza was consumed that this would be their last date.

Andy took Judi home and decided to spend the night in Raleigh since it was already II:00.

On the fifth day he arose late and ate breakfast leisurely. He stopped by the state park in Goldsboro on his way home and watched the small crowd swim. The winding paths along the river and the solitude were soothing.

GOODBYE

Into the distance I see him go,
Ample regret his legacy.
But then again it's okay,
I'll not ask this stranger to stay.

His cadence is sure.
The changing seasons,
Though forever young,
Relentlessly call, "Hut two".

There was a time when we were close,
An innocent time when he was me.
Young we were and carefree.
Did I leave him or he leave me?

Faithful friend or bitter foe?
He taught bountifully of both,
The lessons learned a hefty load,
And a singular treasury.

He made me promises, some he kept;
Others were crushed in an avalanche.
His best offerings a delight, but,
His memory is only bittersweet.

Even if invited, He would not stay,
His departure assured,
So I must say,
Goodbye to Yesterday.

On the sixth day Andy hollered through the screen door from the porch to his mom, "I'm going to meander down to Alvin's place. I might spend the night."

"Won't you be lonely? No one there now."

"If I get too lonely, I'll come on back."

"Well, it's yours now. Your father took Alvin's will and had it probated. As I told you in my letter, Alvin left everything to you. We had to sell all of his critters though. We took the cows to market. Mr. Stevens bought the chickens. Toby was happy to buy the dogs. His old pickup and everything else is still there just like he left it. Your dad also put a gate across the cart path to keep vandals out. I'll get the key for the gate. The old house is not even locked."

Bess retrieved the key for the gate.

"You know Alvin's grave is under that big old oak tree in the back part of his pasture. That's where he directed that he be buried."

"I'll be back," Andy hollered as he walked off.

When he walked by Toby's house, Andy was almost startled. Trailing behind Toby's beagles who had come to bark at him was a dog which looked exactly like Doonsie. Toby followed after the dogs to say hello to Andy.

Andy didn't wait for Toby to say anything. "Toby, that dog looks exactly like Doonsie," Andy said excitedly.

"He ought to," Toby responded. "That Doonsie of yours got to one of my beagles somehow. Naturally she had her biggest litter ever. Seven. Gave all of them away except that one. Nobody seems to want him. His hair is long. Not like a beagle."

"You're trying to get rid of him?" Andy was hopeful. He played and talked with the dog. The dog even had many of Doonsie's mannerism. "What's his name?"

"Haven't even named him. Been around here two years and I haven't even named him. Take him if you want him."

"Thank you, Toby," Andy said as he continued to pat the dog.

"You don't have to thank me. I ought to thank you." Toby paused and finally said, "I'm glad to have you back, Andy." Toby shook Andy's hand.

"Thanks, Toby. I'm glad to be back."

Toby sensed that Andy was going to Alvin's place. "I sure was sorry about Alvin. I really miss him, even if he did have the best trained dogs."

Andy noted that he had never seen Toby self-deprecating before. He seemed older, more self-assured. "I know, Toby. That's where I'm going now. It's not going to be the same with him gone."

As Andy began to walk away, he didn't have to whistle for the dog to follow. He tagged along.

"Looks like he has taken right to you, Andy. Probably because he didn't receive much attention around here."

"Thanks again, Toby." He and his new friend walked off together.

"First thing I've got to do is get you a name. I could call you Doonsie, but you'd have some big shoes to fill, or maybe paws to follow. Let's think about it for a little bit."

The dog listened when Andy spoke. Just like Doonsie. He wouldn't let go of a stick without some friendly growling. Just like Doonsie. He waddled when he walked. Just like Doonsie.

"I'm not going to call you Doonsie. When I hear that name, I want to think of my growing-up years with a good dog. I'll call you Ditto because you remind me so much of Doonsie. You'll have your own name. How's that?"

Ditto lowered his head. Just like Doonsie.

Andy gave him a pat to excuse his lack of response. Ditto appreciated the pat. Just like Doonsie. Andy felt better after talking with him. Just like with Doonsie.

The Old Place

Andy unlocked the gate his father had placed across the cart path leading to Alvin's place. The gate had kept out vandals since most would not want to walk the mile to the house. Andy decided he would leave it open when he was staying at the old place. Except for a few extra weeds and fallen limbs, it appeared the same. It never was much to look at.

"Have you ever been here, Ditto?" Andy asked as he took a chair by the shelter where Alvin had done his cooking.

He assumed his thinking position with feet stretched outward and hands behind his head. He closed his eyes, leaned back in the chair and listened. He could almost hear the echoes and smell the scent of a thousand memories. They flooded his mind. He had to purposely focus to remember any one in particular. He remembered dogs barking in the distance at a treed raccoon. A crackling fire. Nightfall sitting by the fire. Boiling collards. Frying sausage and eggs. A ripple in the water where a fish had broken the still surface. Grandpa's holler just up the river when he made his dive. The excited sounds of children playing catch. A beagle pack after a rabbit. The sound of an ax on a lightwood stump. The smell of the lightwood. Hunting hen eggs. A snapping twig while trying to creep through the woods when squirrel hunting. Squirrels chattering. Oak acorns and hickory nuts falling through tree leaves to the ground after being chewed by squirrels. Dew so thick on the tree limbs that it would condense and fall to the ground like rain. Frost so thick it looked like snow. Honeysuckle flowers. An afternoon sun in the fall of year so bright over your shoulder that the whole world appears a shade of gold. Gentle breezes on a hot day. A day with absolutely nothing to do all day long.

"It's a little intoxicating, Ditto," he said as he opened his eyes.

He got up and strolled around. He went down by the river and lamented again the way it appeared. "I sure wish they hadn't destroyed the river, Ditto."

He went to the back side of the pasture where Alvin was buried. He stood by his grave. "Thank you for this place, Alvin. It will always be special to me."

He returned to the house and found Alvin's supply of pork and beans and sardines. He opened a can of sardines for Ditto and pork and beans for himself. The food was in good shape. They ate and quietly watched another sunset. He slept on the porch of the old house on an army surplus sleeping bag covered by a mosquito net. He watched the night sky quietly display its panorama until he fell asleep. Ditto slept under the net with him.

On the seventh day he arose early to a sparkling morning.

"Ditto, you've got a choice for breakfast. Beans or sardines. Which will it be?" Andy opened sardines for himself and Ditto and observed the morning around him as he ate. A mockingbird was announcing its presence. Andy listened. He watched. "Ditto, have you noticed that mockingbird singing? He doesn't even know where his breakfast will come from, and he's still singing." Andy paused. "And look at that honeysuckle climbing the fence. The sun may scorch it, but it still blossoms." Andy paused. "But you and I know that today the mockingbird will be fed and the blossom will live to provide us with its beauty." He paused. "Do you think there is a lesson here, Ditto?" He paused again. "Maybe so. But today let's just enjoy the beauty." The cumulative effect of the morning and the preceding week with its slower pace, gentle helloes and good-byes, Ditto, and a good night's rest in a quiet place had done wonders for Andy. The feeling was almost miraculous, Andy thought. Some inner strength had been tapped just by plodding along and enduring. He filed the experience away in his memory bank as one of those gentle showers Alvin had talked about. It was not, he decided, just simply some sort of psychological adjustment.

Andy arose and washed his face under the water flow from the hand pump. He stretched and surveyed his surroundings with his new feeling of awareness.

"This place has possibilities, Ditto. Not much but some," Andy smiled.

"The first thing we can do is turn some bantam chickens loose around here. They'll fend for themselves, and we can have a few fresh eggs when we are here. We will do the same with some goats. They'll feed themselves, and we can have some fresh milk. We'll come by and feed them just often enough to make them friendly. We'll fix the roof on the old house and see how long it stands before finally collapsing. We'll throw some cement blocks in the river and cover them with cement and make us a 'rock' to form a washed out hole to swim in. Lots of things we can do around here, Ditto. Are you willing to help?"

Ditto gave his best 'Doonsie' response and received his reassuring pat.

"But today we will rest."

DAWNING

We can sweep up the glass,
From shattered dreams,
Of what might have been,
And dream of unbroken perfection.

We can dry all of our tears,
And suffer the hurt,
And still find tenderness enough,
To cry and ease the pain.

We can bind the wounds,
From ridicule, derision, and mockery,
And neglect the ugly scars,
With healing from deep within.

We can savor the good times,
As a sweet smelling ointment,
And reject the rest,
And hope for better days.

We can watch youthful innocence,
Betrayed by experience,
Or worn with advancing age,
And still trust in ideals.

We can stumble when tested,
Disappoint ourselves,
Forgive our own trespasses,
And rise to strive for excellence.

We can retire in utter defeat,
To a night as dark as pitch,
Rest in peaceful slumber,
And awake to renewed vigor.

We can see love lost;
Our treasures ransacked;
All that we hold dear perish,
And still believe in adventure.

We can groan with all of creation,
For paradise lost to yesterday,
And set our course to the winds,
In search of paradise regained.

We can endure all manner of adversity,
And assert with confidence not of ourselves,
But in Providence Who delights in mornings ---
Tomorrow is another day.

A RETREAT

Andy began the new week with enthusiasm. He tried to start the old pickup truck. Nothing happened when he hit the starter.

"Dead as a door nail, Ditto. It at least needs a battery. No telling what else," he said as he got out.

"Tags are expired too. Let's walk back to Dad's and borrow some transportation."

They took the scenic route. Andy pulled off his shoes and shirt and waded up the river. Ditto enjoyed frolicking in the water as Andy tried to splash him.

"Mom," Andy hollered through the screen door, "I need to borrow your car again."

"The keys are on the kitchen table. How did the old place look?"

"About like usual. Looks like it may fall down any minute. I'm going to do a little work around there. See if I can make it livable."

"I don't think you can do that unless you tear the whole thing down and start over."

"It's not quite that bad. I can at least make it waterproof by putting shingles on top. Those old wood shingles are worn out. Mom, do you know where the title to the old pickup is? It needs tags and I'll need the title."

"No, as a matter of fact, we didn't find any of Alvin's important papers except for his will. It was laid out, kind of like he had been reading it or wanted us to find it."

Andy returned to Alvin's place.

"Ditto, where would Alvin store the title to his truck?" Andy asked as he looked around. "Where is his discharge and the deed to his land? We've got to think like Alvin, you know. That's a pretty hard assignment since nobody knew what Alvin was thinking."

Andy looked in all the obvious places. Under the mattress. He felt for anything which might be inside the mattress. He looked in the old attic. There was one old trunk there, but it contained only worn clothes. He went outside and sat down.

"I just don't believe anything is hidden in that house, Ditto. I think we would have found it. Must be hidden outside. Maybe in the barn."

As Andy sat thinking and looking around, his eyes focused on the brick grate where Alvin did his cooking, and he remembered an incident which had occurred years before. When Alvin had sold a dog to Toby, he had walked over to the grate and removed a brick where he then placed the money Toby had given him.

"I believe we're getting warm, Ditto. You know there's an old hiding place somewhere around this grate," Andy said as he began to search for loose bricks. "I saw Alvin put some money in here a long time ago."

All of the bricks appeared loose, but Andy finally found one that he could remove. Sure enough, there was a space revealed when the brick was removed. Andy peered in.

"I see something in there, Ditto. Got to be a little careful though. Some of those things may be alive."

Andy found a stick to poke through the hole and feel around.

"Nothing seems to be alive, Ditto. Should we stick our hand in there?"

Before he stuck his hand in, he discovered that other bricks could be removed. When they were removed, a very large space, which was full of jars, was revealed. Many of the jars were full of money. Some contained official looking papers.

When Andy had completed his two-hour inventory, he had Alvin's deed, his army discharge, his birth certificate, the pickup truck title, some old unopened letters from someone named Kathleen, and $57,780.00. Andy calculated that Alvin had averaged saving over $2,000.00 each year since his discharge.

"Well! What do you think of that, Ditto? Looks like we can afford a new battery. But for now, let's just put it all back inside. It's been safe all these many years. No reason to think it won't be safe now."

Andy did buy a battery and, to his surprise, the old truck started. He trimmed some limbs from his cart path, fixed his roof, leveled the privy, built a cement 'rock' in the river which, in time, created a small swimming hole, mowed his pasture, bought some bantam chickens and goats, and generally spruced up the place.

After three weeks Andy declared, "Ditto, this place is now too good-looking not to have an official name. What do you think?" Andy reflected. "I wouldn't quite call it an estate." Andy reflected. "How about retreat? It is my retreat." Andy reflected. "Since time does not much matter around here, let's call it *TimeNot*, *TimeNot Retreat*.

Andy found two old boards, heated the fire poker in his fire, and burned and carved the name *TimeNot* on the boards. He posted one at the entrance to Alvin's place on the paved road and the other on the porch post of the old house.

"We now own a retreat, Ditto."

ONE MAN'S EXPLANATION

After six weeks Andy decided he needed a haircut. His military haircut had become a stylish shag.

"Ditto," Andy said as he looked at his image in the mirror hanging on the tree, "I look like one of those hippies you see on TV. You could turn me upside down and mop the floor. As a matter of fact, it looks like someone did mop the floor with me."

He had a rough time trying to get a comb through it.

"I reckon I need a haircut." He grabbed a hand full and pulled it to see how long it was. "I don't necessarily want to make a statement with the shape or length of my hair. --- It seems to me that if you can make your statement just by using the length of your hair, you don't have much of a statement. --- And the same can be said for short hair. --- Maybe Laney can help us out. --- I wonder if the same old crowd gathers at the barber shop every Friday afternoon like they used to."

When Andy arrived at the barber shop, he was not surprised. Toby and Mr. Stevens were there. Laney was in his barber chair in a backward leaning position, waiting.

"Come right in, Andy. It's good to see you," Laney said as he arose and rubbed eyes which had been closed. He would swear he hadn't been asleep, but the sleepy eyes gave him away. A TV was on in the corner but with the sound turned so low it could not be understood.

Everyone greeted Andy.

"You want a haircut, Andy?" Laney asked.

"Yep," Andy said as he climbed into the barber chair, "but just sort of shape it up. I don't want it real short."

"Oh, I see. You don't want a haircut. You want it styled. Don't anyone just want a haircut these days?" Laney said with mock ridicule.

Everyone laughed.

"Well, I want to be at home with you folks here and with my hippie friends. I don't want my hair to speak so loudly that no one hears what I'm saying."

"I never thought of it that way. I think you have a point there. I'll style it then," Laney said as he grasped his scissors and comb daintily and began to trim with mock precision.

Everyone laughed again.

"You know what's happened to the world, don't you?" Laney asked as he trimmed.

"I can tell you exactly," Laney continued without a response from anyone. "Things used to be so simple, so innocent. I guess you could say we were all naive around here, but I certainly enjoyed our blissful ignorance."

Everyone settled in for one of Laney's stories.

"It was all so innocent to be so catastrophic."

Laney took a deep breath.

"In the l950's there was a summer Sunday afternoon in the Jarman's Forks area like Sundays had been, I thought, forever. Right out of a Norman Rockwell painting. If you had to describe this afternoon in one word, it would be 'lazy'. Dog days and all that, you know. The sun shining so bright you'd have to squint unless you had friends or relatives from Up North who had taught you about and provided you with a set of sunglasses."

Everyone smiled.

"Is this going to be one of those tall tales?" Toby asked.

"No, no." Laney assured everyone. "Just listen. You'll agree it's probably true."

He took another deep breath.

"The haze was so thick and hot the tobacco rows appeared to be dancing the further into the distance they stretched. You all know how long they appear when you bend over and begin to crop those lugs. I think you'll all agree that that's where the word 'infinity' probably came from. For any of you not familiar with tobacco, lugs are the first cropping of tobacco which comes from the very bottom of the stalk. Tips are the last cropping at the top of the stalk."

"We know all that, Laney. Get on with your story," Toby said impatiently.

"Well, some present may have forgotten. You know Andy's been gone for some time."

"I remember it well, Laney. Lugging tobacco is something you don't forget," Andy answered.

Laney continued. "Well, like Andy said, you probably don't forget. Lugging is stressful to the back if it's done the way it was then. Just bend over and pull it off. You all probably remember that cropper for Ben Williams who actually disappeared. Rumors persist to this day that he is still undergoing perpetual physical therapy treatment so that he can learn to walk upright again. The truth is he probably caught a ride at the end of the row to anywhere far away and just decided to never come back."

Everyone smiled.

“Anyway, the temperature was pushing l00. If you could get the snakes to leave, everyone would bust Jack Island swimming hole wide open before the day was finished. I didn't know it then, but things were, well, just innocent. And there was certainly no hint that the beginning of the end of those days was about to take place."

Laney took another deep breath.

"It was a good day for a baseball game. Back then there was a field where the motel is now located. A perfect place for a game except for the light pole in centerfield. Travis, Elton's boy, gathered enough boys for the game. That meant raising $.50 to $I.00 for the two or three gallons of $.27-per-gallon gas for the pickup truck to make the rounds. He picked up Dwight. Then Darryl, then Ronnie, Jimmy, Bennie, Lois, Maurice, J.V., Haywood, Sam, Orlando, Jackie, Billy, another Billy, and Emma Lou. Emma Lou you say? Yes, because she could play, and she wasn't even packing a court order."

Everyone laughed.

"Finally they got together I4 players or so. Maurice could knock the first baseman over from third base. J.V. could knock the ball to Richlands. Ronnie could throw with either hand. Nothing got by Darryl at shortstop. One Billy played right field and everybody, including Billy, hoped the ball was never hit in his direction. Jackie could pitch. I understand he actually tried out for the Brooklyn Dodgers but some class 'B' team hit I4 straight home runs off him in his first practice game. He runs an insulation business somewhere in Western North Carolina now. Those I4 straight home runs are still an unofficial record to this day."

It was time for everyone to laugh again.

"I'm going to lay all the blame for what happened on that light pole in centerfield. One had to be awfully careful when shagging flies to avoid this pole. Bennie was not careful enough. Thank goodness he was not running full out but was sort of drifting over to catch the ball when the collision occurred. It was enough to put a knot on the right side of his head and lay him out flat. He jumped up quick enough, but funny things began to happen. In the confusion to see if he was all right, someone put his hat on backwards. Someone else felt of his head and told him he felt cool and clammy. Someone else yelled, "Your hat". Bennie misunderstood and thought someone had called him a cat. He knew he felt cool. So he's now running around in centerfield yelling, 'I'm a cool cat'."

Laney now had everyone's attention.

"Would you believe it caught on and hold onto your safety belts. The very next Sunday everyone is wearing their hat backwards and talking about what 'cool cats' they were. It spread all over like a brush fire on a windy day. Some fellow with a guitar as far away as Mississippi picked up what those Jarman's Forks boys started, swiveled his hips, went singing on television, and made a million dollars. Everybody in the country wanted to be a 'cool cat'."

"Elvis," said Toby while smiling. "The boy's name from Mississippi was Elvis Presley."

"I know that, Toby. I just wanted to make sure you weren't sleeping."

Laney continued. "Now what's cool today ain't cool tomorrow so things have to keep changing. And the origin of and trail from 'cool cat' is not as clear to most historians, but I'm absolutely and fully convinced, and ain't nobody going to change my mind, that that's why today we have men with hair down their back, haircuts that convince you the barber was blindfolded, whole songs where you can't understand one single word, and unless I should offend anybody else, I'll just say etceteras."

Everyone had another good laugh.

"You can laugh if you want to," Laney continued tongue-in-cheek. "And there you have it. Innocence, simplicity gone like a puff of smoke! Trampled! Killed by accident! Ooooooh, I long for the good old days. If only that light pole hadn't been in centerfield, I could be standing around here in my blissful ignorance giving haircuts instead of styling hair."

"Laney, I do believe you could solve all of the world's problems if folks would just listen to you." Toby closed the conversation with a laugh.

Andy realized again he was glad to be home.

THE TRAVELER'S HOME?

It was fall and time for harvesting. Andy helped Mr. Stevens gather his corn. Mr. Stevens gave Andy enough corn to fill the old crib at *TimeNot*. It took two loads of Alvin's pickup truck to fill the crib. He could grab four to six ears of corn and heave them into the crib. As Andy was throwing the last load into the crib, he heard a vehicle coming down the cart path to *TimeNot*. He sat down on the tailgate and waited to see who would appear.

"Who do you think this might be, Ditto?"

A pickup truck came into view. It had six-foot high racks attached to the bed and a canvas top covering the racks. The contents were not visible. A man got out of the pickup. He wore dark blue denim bell-bottom trousers and a blue shirt. The clothes were clean. His shoes were polished. He removed a sailor's hat which he had been wearing turned down. Andy could see his face more clearly. Time had etched its passing therein with deep wrinkles. It was clean and shaven. His hair was full with more gray than not. The remaining hair was brown. He was slender. Andy guessed the man to be in excess of 70 years of age. But Andy could detect a sparkle in his eyes which suggested a youthful exuberance that had not succumbed to time's onslaught. He moved slowly but gracefully, even stately. Andy had never seen him before.

"Would you like some assistance?" the man asked as he approached Andy. His enunciation was clear and concise.

"Don't mind if I do," Andy replied.

The man looked at Andy's position for a moment and finally asked, "Are you loading or unloading?"

He smiled.

"I wouldn't want to be throwing in while you're throwing out or vice versa."

Andy returned his smile.

"Unloading."

They threw the remaining corn into the crib. The old gentleman took a few deep breaths and unbuttoned the top button of his shirt for cooling.

"Most people call me Sailor Dan, or Sailor, or just Dan. Whichever you like. Or whatever you like. I have been called worse." He offered his hand.

They shook hands.

Andy was slow to answer as usual, and the questions in his mind must have been evident on his face.

"There is no reason you should know me," the old man explained.

"Oh, I'm glad to hear that. You had me wondering. You seem to belong here."

Andy realized he had not introduced himself.

"I'm Andy."

"Yes, I know your name."

Andy's face must have again reflected his puzzlement.

"I asked around town."

Andy shook his head as if he were beginning to understand.

"That's Ditto at your feet trying to make friends."

"Hello, Ditto."

He examined Ditto and said, "I'd say our pedigrees are similar. Questionable."

He gave Ditto a good patting.

"No insult intended."

"You can't insult Ditto. He just keeps coming back for more."

Andy wondered why the man had asked about him.

"You learned my name by asking around town?"

"Oh, yes, I retired a while back after stints with the U.S. Navy and Merchant Marines. Since then I just travel on my own. When I arrive at a new town I look for the most interesting character I can find. I've met hobos, alcoholics, recluses, lunatics, philosophers, and some who don't even deserve mention. Some would not let me in the door. I can't say I blame them."

He waited for Andy to absorb what he had said.

"Your name came to fore in Richlands. In the interesting category, by the way, not any of those others."

"Well, I'm glad to hear that." Andy smiled.

"They said you spend ample time here by yourself. They also said you do more thinking than talking."

"That pretty well sums it up," Andy admitted. "I have heard said that there are three kinds of people in the world. Those who make things happen, those who watch things happen, and those who wonder what happened. I suppose I'm in the middle category trying not to slip into the latter."

They both smiled. Rapport between them was evident and growing.

"I suspect that if you attentively watch for a sufficient time, you will move to the former."

Sailor Dan liked Andy. Andy liked Sailor Dan.

"Would you like to swap old sea stories?" Sailor Dan asked.

"Certainly. Pull up a chair," Andy said inviting Sailor Dan to stay.

"First things first. I haven't had a bath in three days. I notice the creek over there. Is it permissible to take a bath before the sun goes down?"

"Okay by me. But you're going to find it chilly."

Andy had stopped taking baths in the river some five weeks before.

"I've bathed in colder."

Sailor Dan returned to his pickup truck and began unfolding the canvas covering the truck. Andy helped. They unfolded and set poles until the back of the pickup appeared to be a tent with a pickup under it. A folding chair placed under the 'tent' made it appear homey. Sailor Dan went down to the river to take a bath.

Andy heated some water and took his bath inside the old house. He then cooked their evening meal over the open fire. They ate near the warmth of the fire. *TimeNot* was conducive to thoughtful conversation. They talked. They talked of humility, pride, and time. They talked of spiritual matters. They swapped old sea stories.

Andy glanced toward Alvin's grave and thought that Alvin would have enjoyed the setting. He would also have contributed his curtly stated opinion at the appropriate, or maybe inappropriate, interval.

"Tell me about *TimeNot*."

"I come here to be with my thoughts," Andy replied. "Thoughts I can't quite grasp elsewhere. It is my retreat from distractions, my retreat from time."

"And a myriad of distractions we have," Sailor Dan said in agreement.

He paused to consider.

"I take mine with me," he said. "My *TimeNot* goes with me."

Andy assumed he was talking about his pickup truck home. But Sailor Dan continued.

"I'll tell you a story," Sailor Dan began.

Andy listened.

"As I have told you, I was in the navy. During general quarters, or battle stations, all doors, hatches if you desire to be technically correct, are closed and secured tightly. They are water-tight. That, of course, is to protect the integrity of the ship, its wholeness. If one compartment is ruptured and floods, the ship will continue to float because of the water-tight integrity of the remaining compartments. If two are flooded, the ship will continue to float. And so on. It will finally begin to list. And there will come a time, if so many compartments are flooded, when the ship will sink."

Sailor Dan collected his thoughts and continued.

"Protect *TimeNot*'s integrity, Andy. And when you have sailed the seven seas and dropped anchor for the last time, you will find that in protecting *TimeNot*, you will have built *TimeNot*."

Both were quiet.

"Mr. Dan, we're not talking about a place any more, are we?"

"No, Andy."

Sailor Dan retired to his 'tent'. Andy listened as he played taps on a bugle. The sound was distinct in the still night. It suggested rest, a restful sleep, soldiers' graveyards, and that eternal rest.

"Lights out, Andy," Mr. Dan called.

"Mr. Dan, I'll see you in the morning," Andy replied. He retired to the old house.

In the morning it is," Mr. Dan called back.

Andy considered Sailor Dan's story. He then remembered nights of curing tobacco with his grandpa and some conversations with him. Those recollections were pleasant.

His thoughts lastly turned once more to a girl he had yet to know. Those expectations were pleasant. He was contented.

They ate breakfast together the next morning. Sailor Dan, with Andy's help, packed his pickup truck. He shook Andy's hand and hugged him with a pat on the back.

He left.

Andy hoped he would see him again.

Andy was becoming a little more serious about finding a job. For three months he had been enjoying his sabbatical. He had learned to play golf at a little-nine-hole course in Kenansville. He had done some fishing with his dad. He had spruced up *TimeNot*. He had even thought about accepting Alvin's mantle and continuing his monastic existence at *TimeNot*.

"Looks like the weather is going to get a little serious about turning cooler," Mr. Greene said as he and Andy drank their Pepsis under Mr. Greene's store shelter.

It was late fall. The tree leaves were shades of brown, red, yellow, and orange. Many had fallen to the ground and the cool, brisk breeze had blown a few into a pile around Andy's feet and rocking chair.

"Yes, it does," Andy responded. "It's about that time of year. I always enjoy the changing seasons though."

"And so do I." Mr. Greene took a swallow of his Pepsi. "Are you still looking for a job, Andy?"

"Yes, and I may have found one. The telephone company is interested because of my communications training in the army. They say they will be hiring the first of the year."

"That would be a nice job. I expect it pays pretty good, especially for these parts. Not that many good jobs around here right now."

"I haven't even asked them about the pay. I figure they will pay what I'm worth."

"Well, don't give your services away. Right now, everybody who has a phone around here is on a ten-party line. The lines don't even reach half the people. They are going to need to put quite a few more lines in, and they'll be needing more help."

"You're right about that. The company is a growing concern. I hope I can get on with them."

They both watched as Tyler Brinson drove up to the gas tanks. Tyler was Toby's oldest boy.

"Fill her up, Mr. Greene. I'm off to Greenville, or Raleigh, or Chapel Hill or somewhere to apply for college."

"You don't even know where you are going to apply?" Mr. Greene asked as he pumped the gas.

"I'd love to go to the university in Chapel Hill. I don't know if I have the grades though. I think I'll put in applications any place they will let me."

"Are you going off to college already, Tyler?" Andy asked. "It just doesn't seem like you ought to be that old. You were just a little fellow when I went off to the army."

"Yes, I hope to go next year. I'm a senior right now."

"That will be $3.25, Tyler. She's full as a tick now. That ought to take you there and back."

Tyler paid Mr. Greene.

"Are you still staying at Alvin's place, Andy?" Tyler asked.

"Part time," Andy replied. "And some with my dad."

"I saw that sign at the entrance. What does *TimeNot* mean?"

"It's just a name I thought up. I just wanted to give the place some character."

"You didn't have to worry about that. It has always had character. How did you come up with *TimeNot*?"

"Time just doesn't seem to matter around there. It's my name for time not mattering much."

"Have you thought about college?"

"It's crossed my mind. I have some army benefits available if I decide to go. But right now, I think I'm going to work for the telephone company."

"Come on and ride with me if you want to. You can think about it on the way."

Andy thought for a minute. "I believe I'll just do that. I'll even pay half your gas bill."

"You don't have to worry about the gas. I'll enjoy having you along."

Andy got in with Tyler and off they went. They came to the fork in the road with Greenville in one direction and Chapel Hill in the other. Tyler pulled off on the shoulder of the road and asked, "Which will it be?"

"If you want to go to the university in Chapel Hill, you ought to shoot for that," Andy answered.

"Chapel Hill it is," Tyler said as he made a left turn.

They arrived in Chapel Hill at noon and found the admissions office.

"So, you want to attend the University of North Carolina?" the clerk at the window asked.

"Yes, ma'am," Tyler answered.

"How about your friend?"

Tyler turned to Andy. "How about it, Andy? Want to apply?"

Andy gave it some thought as usual. "Might as well," he finally said.

The clerk handed each of them an application. Tyler and Andy completed their applications and submitted them to the clerk.

They then surveyed the campus. The Bell Tower, the Old Well, Kenan Stadium, Carmichael Auditorium, and Franklin Street were all impressive sights for Tyler who had not done much traveling. They were on their way home by 3:30 p.m. Andy could not pass the state park in Goldsboro without asking Tyler to stop. The park was such a pretty place even in the winter. They stood on the cliffs along the river and enjoyed the view.

They returned home.

The Telephone Company Calls

Andy did go to work for the telephone company. His supervisor's name was Jimmy Johnson. His first day was spent being introduced to everyone and pulling some wires on the main frame which connected the incoming individual telephone subscriber lines to the office equipment.

On the second day Mr. Johnson stood in the central telephone equipment office with Andy and one more person.

"Do the two of you know each other?" Mr. Johnson asked.

"No, sir," they responded in unison.

"Andy Goodday, meet Hank Crowell."

They shook hands.

"Hank was supposed to start yesterday with you, but his dad was hospitalized. Andy, you introduce him to everyone when you get a chance."

"Yes, sir," Andy responded.

"Your assignment today is to clean these switches."

Mr. Johnson then demonstrated the correct method, asked if there were any questions, and left when neither asked anything.

"I hope you dad will be okay," Andy said.

"We are all hoping too."

Andy waited to give Hank a chance to talk about his dad if he desired. When Hank said nothing more, Andy pointed at the switches and said, "Have you ever seen so many of just one thing?"

"Only in one of those situations where mirrors are facing each other and the reflections reach on into infinity," Hank said.

"It kind of reminds me of tobacco rows on a hot August day. They reach to infinity too."

They smiled.

"There are 5,000 of them. Five hundred in each bay and ten bays. I counted them," Andy said.

"Nothing like getting started in order to finish a job," Hank said.

"Let's go," Andy suggested.

For three hours they cleaned switches with not a word between them. Mr. Johnson came by at ll:00.

"Have you fellows had a break yet?" Mr. Johnson asked.

"No, sir," they responded in unison.

"Well, we don't expect you to clean all of these switches in one day. Take a break. Fifteen minutes. We normally take our morning break at l0:00."

Mr. Johnson noted their enthusiasm and the number of switches they had cleaned. "Looks like you are making good progress. Keep it up."

They smiled and went to the lounge for a soft drink.

"So. This is just your second day?" Hank said.

"Yes, I have been loafing since I got out of service back last summer. Finally decided I had better find a job."

"Hey, I was in the service too," Hank replied.

They exchanged background information. Andy told Hank about himself. Andy learned that Hank had also served in Vietnam. He had moved to Jacksonville because his father was in the marines and had returned after his service time. He already had some college and planned to return to school. They liked each other.

They completed the cleaning of the 5,000 switches in just over three days and were sent to a small satellite office to do some cleaning there. James Byrd was assigned to permanently man and maintain the office. He had planned to take the afternoon off. After showing Hank and Andy how to clean the equipment, he departed. Andy and Hank were alone in the office. The office was new and automated. No problems were expected. They were about their business of cleaning when the office suddenly became quiet. The sounds of relays clicking and switches activating stopped completely. An alarm went off. Andy and Hank looked at each other.

"Makes you kind of want to run outside and get in a bunker," Hank said, recalling his days in Vietnam.

"It sure does," Andy responded. "The main switchboard is over here. Let's see if we can find the trouble."

A blinking red light was obvious. It was labeled 'Main Alarm. System failure. Go to Bay 5'. Andy and Hank went to Bay 5. There was another blinking red light at the end of the bay. The bay was labeled 'Call Processor'. Both began to call upon their experience in communications equipment in the service.

"It looks like everything begins right here," said Hank.

"I'd say so," Andy responded while looking around. "Here are the schematics for the equipment of this wall."

They had just begun to study the schematics when a phone rang on the desk of the main switchboard.

"How did that call get through?" asked Andy.

"Beats me."

Andy answered the phone call. It was their supervisor, Jimmy Johnson.

"What's wrong out there? No one can get through to that exchange."

"We've got a main alarm signal. But how did you get through?" Andy wondered.

"This is a direct line from the downtown office. Where's James? Can't he get it fixed?"

"James is off today. There's no one here except Hank and myself. We're taking a look right now."

"Oh, my gosh. I'd forgotten about James being off." He paused. "But you've not had technical training on that equipment." Mr. Johnson paused. "Well, do the best you can. I'll be there as soon as I can." He paused again. "Don't do any harm."

Hank and Andy returned to the schematic.

"I could think more clearly if that alarm were quiet," Andy said.

Hank found an 'off' switch for the audible alarm. The blinking lights continued.

They checked all fuses at the end of Bay 5. No problem there.

"Since nothing is happening in the whole office, the trouble must be located at the very beginning of the call processing. Let's go to panel I," Hank deduced.

Andy began to pull the covers from panels I, 2, and 3. He probed carefully with a screwdriver to check for loose, burned, over-heated equipment. Nothing was obvious. They listened. They could hear a low-level whine.

"That's a relay trying to engage," Hank said.

Andy agreed.

They circled the panel listening carefully. They both agreed that the whine came from 'RI' relay.

"There's a spare parts cabinet over there," Andy pointed.

After a search they found an 'RI' relay.

"It looks the same to me. What do you think?" Hank questioned.

"It looks the same to me too. But Mr. Johnson said do no harm," Andy said, displaying his always careful approach to any problem.

"Let's do it," Hank said as he reached inside the equipment and carefully unplugged 'RI'.

"Well, at least the office didn't blow up," Andy smiled.

Hank held the relays side by side. "They're the same," he said confidently.

He inserted the new 'RI'. The office immediately came to life. The familiar clicking sounds of calls being processed returned.

They smiled at each other.

When Mr. Johnson arrived, he was pleasantly surprised. He reset the alarms and declared the office back to normal. He did not try to hide his approval of their actions.

"Looks like you fellows have earned your keep. And this is only your first week with us."

Telephone Basketball

The telephone company had a basketball team which competed in the Jacksonville City League. Andy and Hank played. Referees were usually provided by the city, but on one occasion they did not show. The teams agreed to play the game and allow the players involved to call their own fouls. The game was close. Near its end Hank and number 22 from the opposing team chased a ball out of bounds. The team gaining possession would be in a good position to win the game. The teams began arguing. There was some shoving. Andy and Hank watched. Everyone finally turned to Hank and number 22 for an answer.

Hank waited.

"It's our ball," said number 22.

Hank tossed the ball to number 22 without a word. Two nights later Hank and Andy were working late and cutting in some new equipment. They talked about the out-of-bounds situation.

"Hank, I saw clearly that out-of-bounds call between you and number 22 Tuesday night. It was your ball."

"You're right, it was my ball."

"Why didn't you argue about the call?"

"I had a couple of reasons."

"Well, are you going to tell me?" Andy asked after some waiting.

"Yeah, I just settled this issue in my own mind a few years back and I'm trying to remember." He continued. "First of all, when you compete, not only in sports, but in any endeavor, you win when you do the best you can. And that's true regardless of the score. The competition only provides the setting. If some opponent has pounded you mercilessly, examine your performance afterwards, and if you've done the best you can, you win. Even if you're missing an ear."

They smiled.

"Second, the substance of a man's character is defined by its lowest common denominator. If we get upset and argue over trifles, how are we ever going to get around to dealing with weightier matters?"

They pulled wires and soldered connections in silence.

"By the way, Andy, why didn't you argue over the call?"

"It was your call," Andy said with a shrug of the shoulders.

Hank shook his head, indicating he understood.

Andy did not ask about 'weightier' matters at the time. He was confident that Hank had a keen sense of 'weighty'. They would later talk on many occasions of weighty matters. There was never a difference of opinion which could not be reconciled in an unencumbered discussion.

They would later go on double dates together. Andy would arrange for Hank to have a date with his cousin. Hank would fix Andy a date with a friend of a friend. They ate pizza together. They fished together. They became friends.

Then in May, Andy received notice that he had been accepted to the University of North Carolina at Chapel Hill. Tyler was also accepted. Andy made arrangements with the telephone company for a leave of absence and enrolled in September.

He often wondered about the seemingly fortuitous nature of his decision to go to college. Was it really chance? On a quiet day at *TimeNot* he discussed the matter with Ditto.

"Ditto, you know I'm going off to college in a week. You'll have to take care of *TimeNot* for me. I'm not sure I hadn't just as soon stay here with you."

They enjoyed the quiet.

"Who decided I should go to college anyway? Did I? Or did Tyler arrive at Mr. Greene's store at the appointed time?"

Andy and Ditto considered the question.

"Now be serious, Ditto. Is this old universe random or ordered?"

Andy was emphatic.

Ditto knew he was more involved and managed a wag of his tail.

They again considered the question.

Andy closed the conversation with his conclusion. "To each his own, Ditto, but I suspect that fate is design gone awry."

THE COLLEGE YEARS

Andy approached college as he did other endeavors. He did a lot of listening. He performed the assigned task and observed. He attended one basketball game and two football games. He played golf at Finley Golf Course and basketball in Carmichael Auditorium, Woolen Gym and the Tin Can. He enjoyed the village atmosphere of Chapel Hill which prevailed in the l960's and early l970's. For the most part, students walked or rode bicycles to classes.

He ate at the campus cafeteria when it was necessary to walk through lines of state highway patrolmen. The Patrolmen were protecting those who wanted to eat from those students who were supporting a workers' boycott. It was a time of nationwide campus unrest, particularly over the Vietnam War.

Andy lived off campus in a rented mobile home. He graduated in three calendar years by attending summer classes. It was weekend visits to *TimeNot* and talks with Ditto which helped him maintain a proper perspective during this period of his formal education.

A History Lesson

"Ditto. I got through my first semester with all A's and B's. That ought to help me with my GPA if I have a bad semester," Andy said on one of his quiet weekends at *TimeNot*. "You know, we studied western civilization. We covered some six thousands years of recorded history." Andy paused. "You know what impressed me the most?" Andy paused. "Every king, every Caesar, every tyrant, every benevolent leader, every country, every kingdom, all had a beginning date, or birth date, and an ending date, or death date. They all had a beginning and an end. They wrote their stories, some more grand than others, and passed on." Andy paused. "Ditto, you and I will write our little stories and pass on." Andy paused. "Does anyone take note of our deeds? Does anyone take note of our passing? Does posterity care?" Andy paused. "Ditto, we may never make copy for a history book, but you and I will know our own deeds. Does anyone else matter?"

The Tyrant's Lesson

"Ditto. Let's talk about tyrants and those subject to them. Of course, the tyrant is a hopeless case. He loves his position of power, or money, or whatever. Who knows what drives a tyrant? Some of his subjects followed willingly and thereby became tyrants themselves. Some subjects resisted and paid with their lives. Where the human spirit endured, it was finally victorious. Ditto, which subject would you rather be? The one who followed or the one who resisted?"

Ditto did his part. He listened.

"Let's say it this way. You're subject to more harm as putty in someone's hands than with his heel upon your neck."

A Character Lesson

"Ditto, I have a professor who dresses and acts the part. He smokes a pipe. He knows his subject matter. He is always ready to engage in a debate regarding his field of learning. I listened to him teach for a semester. I talked with him many times after class. But who is he? To this day, I do not know the man.

Jeanne

Jeanne Rukas was from Cicero which is a suburb of Chicago. She attended the University of North Carolina because she had an aunt who resided in Chapel Hill. Jeanne boarded with her aunt while she attended college. Andy sat next to Jeanne in a history class. The class had been in progress for two weeks.

"Would you like to eat lunch together?" Andy inquired.

They had exchanged glances and some nods of the head over the two-week period.

"That would be nice," Jeanne responded without hesitation.

They became friends.

Each provided the other with a copy of class notes if one missed a class. Andy discovered something of Jeanne's sense of perspective while trying to understand an item from her notes. It read, "Sell hats - Marie - I0/I6/I793." Andy had to ask.

Jeanne responded, "Oh, that. Marie Antionette was beheaded on October I6, I793.

Robust laughter followed.

They attended a basketball game. They ate lunches together. They studied for mid-term exams together. When spring break came, Jeanne invited Andy to spend the week at her home with her parents in Cicero. Andy accepted.

Cicero was a picturesque working class neighborhood with row houses, tree-lined streets, and children playing in the streets. Mr. Rukas liked Andy immediately. He liked Andy's pace and his 'yes, sir' and 'no, sir' responses. Andy quickly became the son Mr. Rukas never had. Mr. Rukas called Andy 'son' in an affectionate manner.

"Son, do all southern boys take life as easily as you?" He asked.

"No, Dad," Jeanne butted in. "Andy's a little unique. But don't tell him I said so," she whispered loudly behind a hand held up between herself and Andy.

"Do they all say 'yes, sir' and 'no, sir'?"

"No, sir, they don't," Andy replied. "And appearances can be deceiving. Life is not always so easy."

When they visited various sites throughout Chicago over the next week, Mr. Rukas would always say, "Let Andy drive." Andy did.

The weather was extremely mild for April in Chicago with temperatures in the 70's. One outing was to a park on Lake Michigan in downtown Chicago for a picnic. A lunch of sandwiches with tea was followed by a stroll along Lake Michigan. Andy could see in the distance a sign which read 'NO SWIMMING'. Now Andy had not thought about swimming until he saw the sign. But the seed had been planted. Memories of Jack Island seemed almost real. The closer he came to the sign the more it suggested, rather than prohibited, a swim. Besides, he was eager to further impress Jeanne's parents with his country boy swimming and diving abilities. By the time he reached the sign his mind was made up. He was going swimming. When he approached the sign, he pulled off his shirt, stood on the 'NO SWIMMNG' sign, and dove into Lake Michigan.

He determined from everyone's comments that he had indeed made an impression.

"Andy, get yourself out of that water. You'll freeze to death," Mrs. Rukas chided.

"Andy, have you lost your mind?" Jeanne yelled. "You'll get us all arrested."

"Son, that sign was not placed there to protect the lake. It was put there to protect you. The water is somewhat polluted, to say the least," Mr. Rukas warned.

Andy quickly decided that Mrs. Rukas' comment deserved the most attention. Just a few short weeks before, the lake was solid ice where Andy was swimming. The water temperature was now 38 degrees. Andy felt as if pins and needles were puncturing his body. He needed to get out of the water, but, for one of the few times in his life, he had not thought the situation through before acting. When he swam to the sea wall, he discovered that it was five feet high with no ladder. Mr. Rukas leaned over the wall and offered Andy a towel. It was too short. Mr. Rukas had to tie three towels together. Andy almost pulled Mr. Rukas into the lake. The towels were finally secured to the 'NO SWIMMING' sign and Andy pulled himself out.

His venture was not complete.

The friendly April breeze now felt as cold as the Siberian Express the weather man often talked about. He began to shiver. He put his shirt back on and wrapped himself in the towels. Ten minutes of warming relieved his physical suffering but not his embarrassment.

"They don't make water that cold Down South," Andy said sheepishly. "Let's just blame all this on misdirected enthusiasm spawned by beautiful spring weather."

"They don't make boys like you in Chicago," Mr. Rukas said. He did not try to conceal his admiration for Andy's youthful daring. He placed his arm around Andy's shoulder and they returned to the picnic area.

Everyone had a hearty laugh.

Charcoaling

The good weather continued and the next day was spent charcoaling steaks in the Rukas' back yard. It was another occasion for embarrassment for Andy.

Mrs. Rukas served drinks from a two-gallon container. Andy thought it was a tasty punch. Over a one-hour period, he drank a large portion of the two gallons. He had remained seated for the period and noticed no effects from his drinking.

Mr. Rukas had watched Andy's consumption with amusement.

When Mrs. Rukas dropped a fork, Andy jumped to his feet to retrieve it. As he leaned down for the fork, his whole world began to spin. He did a flip over his right shoulder, finally coming to rest on his back. He was completely disoriented. He lay still trying to determine what had happened. Everyone rushed to his aid.

"Are you alright?" Jeanne questioned.

"I don't know." Andy was still confused.

"Son, it appears that you may have had too much of Mama's refreshments," Mr. Rukas said with a smile on his face.

"What happened? And what's refreshments got to do with it?"

Andy was now sitting on the ground with his head between his hands.

"Son, I believe you're a little tipsy," Mr. Rukas continued, a bigger smile on his face.

"Tipsy?" Andy tried to think for a moment. "How can that be?"

"Well, I'd say you have had about six glasses of Mama's refreshments." Mr. Rukas laughed.

"It did taste good."

"It's one of her recipes. About twenty-five percent liquor. We should have told you, but I was having too much fun watching." Mr. Rukas still had a big smile on his face as he helped Andy back to his seat.

"I'm sure I appeared quite silly. I'm just not used to alcohol."

Andy collected himself and settled into his chair.

"By the way, did anyone get the license plate number of that fork?" Andy asked.

They all had another good laugh.

Touring

Jeanne gave Andy a tour of Chicago the next two days. They visited a museum. They rode the loop train to Great Lakes Naval Training Center and back. The train ride gave them an opportunity to talk of personal matters. They talked of children, their desires for a home, and where life might lead them. They were searching.

Church

The Rukases were Catholic and everyone went to church on Sunday. Andy seemed to be kneeling when everyone was sitting or standing when everyone was kneeling or sitting when everyone was standing. During his lag period he glanced at Jeanne from the corner of his eye, and they smiled at each other. Andy shrugged his shoulders, indicating he was doing his best. He also thought how angelic Jeanne appeared with the white cover for her head also covering a portion of her forehead.

The History Class Ends

Andy and Jeanne finished the school year studying together. But their lunches were less frequent. Jeanne went home for the summer and Andy continued classes. There were no phone calls or letters during the summer. Andy saw Jeanne once during the following fall semester. She was walking arm-in-arm with some fellow. She quickly let go of his arm when she saw Andy.

"Andy!" she said.

The situation was momentarily awkward.

Jeanne finally began introductions. "This is Brad. We have chemistry together."

Andy nodded.

"And this is Andy. We had history together last semester."

Brad nodded.

They talked further of how they had spent the summer. They talked of other trivial matters. All three wanted the conversation to end as soon as possible. They finally said their good-byes.

"Goodbye, Andy."

"It's never goodbye, Jeanne. I'll see you later."

Andy walked a short distance and turned to look for one last time. Jeanne was doing the same. They waved. Another chapter in each of their lives had been written. Both lamented the loss, not necessarily of each other, but of something that might have been. They would remember.

Andy talked to Ditto about Jeanne one weekend at *TimeNot*.

"Ditto. I had a friend named Jeanne. We had classes together. We studied together. We went to a basketball game. She was, and still is, as pretty as a peach. She was sweet and understanding. She liked pleasing me, and I enjoyed making her happy. She was the best friend I had at school. We walked hand-in-hand for a while, even heart-to-heart. Why did I not love her?"

A Story of Two Dogs

When Andy was to return to *TimeNot* and his dad's within a short period of time, he would occasionally take Ditto to Chapel Hill. Ditto would follow Andy to class and wait outside the door of the classroom building. He would not be distracted from his vigil by passing squirrels or friendly students. He was friendly enough, allowing occasional pats, but his desire was to see Andy appear.

Patrick had a math class with Andy. Patrick also had a dog. The dog's name was Major. Patrick always had Major on a leash and would tie him while he was in class. Patrick would often return to find that Major had slipped his collar over his head and had departed for parts unknown. Andy had helped Patrick find Major on more than one occasion.

"Andy, you bring Ditto to Chapel Hill only occasionally, and he follows you around faithfully without a leash. I keep Major here all the time, and he runs off every chance he gets. How do you explain that?" Patrick asked as he slipped Major's collar back over his head.

"Major's body is bound, Patrick. His heart is elsewhere. Whatever binds Ditto is stronger than chains."

Patrick nodded in agreement.

The Logic Professor

The logic professor accepted no authority but reason. His name was Mr. Lowen. He often said, "If you must quote some authority in an attempt to defend or enhance your position, you have abandoned reason."

Andy was passing through a parking lot on his way to logic class when Professor Lowen got out of a car just ahead.

"Professor Lowen!" Andy called. He ran forward to catch up. They walked along slowly.

"Mr. Goodday, how can you be certain that I am Professor Lowen?"

Andy paused and then responded, "I am as certain that you are Professor Lowen as you are that I'm Mr. Goodday." Andy knew that Professor Lowen enjoyed a good verbal sparring match.

They smiled.

"What's on your mind, Mr. Goodday?"

"I have been thinking about your comment concerning sanity during the last class."

"And which comment might that be?"

"You said, 'If someone has never wondered if he is sane, he probably isn't.' I agree."

"That's generous of you, Mr. Goodday. But it's unusual for me to make an assertion with such clarity. I usually speak in ambiguities. Just food for thought, you understand."

"Well, maybe I paraphrased you."

"And have you decided that you are sane?"

"I have yet to decide, but I did decide this. Sanity is the ability to make sense of the incomprehensible. Insanity is the ability to make sense of the incomprehensible."

Professor Lowen took four steps more and stopped.

"Class begins in five minutes, Mr. Goodday."

Andy went inside the philosophy building and took his seat in the classroom. Professor Lowen was fifteen minutes late. Other students began to wonder if they should leave. Andy assured everyone that he had just seen Professor Lowen and that he was in the building. They waited.

When Professor Lowen did enter the classroom he walked to the blackboard and wrote in quotations:

"*Sanity is the ability to make sense of the incomprehensible. Insanity is the ability to make sense of the incomprehensible.*"

"Does anyone know the source of this paradox?" He asked as the turned to the class.

Everyone remained quiet. Andy slid lower into his seat.

"This is our subject matter for today. You will discover its source at the end of this class."

For the remaining portion of the ninety-minute class Professor Lowen exchanged questions and answers with students. When the bell rang, he walked to the blackboard and wrote "*Andrew Goodday*" at the end of the quote. Everyone turned to look at Andy. Andy slid even lower in his seat.

"Since Mr. Goodday is our authority for the day, he may have the last word. Mr. Goodday." Professor Lowen waved an open hand toward Andy, indicating that he should stand.

Andy arose slowly from what had become a crouched position. He gathered himself and spoke distinctly. Since he was the authority for the day, he would act the part. He said boldly, "Professor Lowen, is everything you are teaching us here, is everything the university is teaching us, nothing more than the incomprehensible which leaves each of us no more able to distinguish the sane from the insane?"

The room was quiet. Students were wondering if Professor Lowen would be offended. Professor Lowen waited. Students did not move. Andy shifted his weight. He wondered if he had played his part too well.

Professor Lowen began to slowly applaud. Students joined him and the pace became more vigorous. When the applause had ceased, the students filed from the classroom leaving Professor Lowen and Andy alone. Andy began to leave.

"I appreciate a student providing me with food for thought, Mr. Goodday." He offered his hand.

They shook hands.

Another Professor

After the seventh semester Andy returned to *TimeNot* for a talk with Ditto. Over a Saturday morning breakfast of sausage and eggs by Alvin's hearth, Andy began in his deliberate pace.

"Ditto. I have a sad story to tell you. I had a professor who had a doctorate in religion. I think he also had other doctoral degrees. I often talked to him after class about the different religions. He could recite the fundamentals of most religions. He had studied the social sciences extensively. He understood the cause and effect of human actions and reaction. He was intelligent. He told me he was an agnostic. We could talk for hours after class about the most complicated of matters, and he was completely rational. I learned a lot from him. But sometime we would be talking and an automobile would go by with a license plate with a certain sequence of digits, and that professor would turn to me and say that the driver of that automobile was looking to kill him. At first, I thought he was joking or trying to test me. But each time he would see a certain sequence, he would repeat the story. I would ask him why, but he would say it was too complicated for me to understand. He would then resume normal behavior. But each time he told the story, I could see that he was becoming more afraid of this imagined killer." Andy paused. "He committed suicide this week."

Andy thought for a long time.

"Ditto, I think this can be said, not just of this situation, but of all of academia. Knowledge alone is not the answer."

Andy continued his reflections and then said to Ditto, "You may gather knowledge with your mind, but you must understand with your heart. Don't we all do that anyway, even if we possess a tremendous amount of knowledge?"

Andy reflected further.

"A smart man understands what he sees. A wise man understands what he feels."

A Fellow on a Bench

Andy had an ll:00 a.m. class. After the class, when the weather was cooperative, he would often eat lunch outside on a bench. An elderly gentleman would occasionally join him. The two of them would talk of everything from politics to the proper consistency for tomato catchup on a sandwich. Their conversations numbered ten over the course of the semester. Andy never learned his name. He never learned of his station at the university. He never saw him again after that one semester. For all that Andy knew, he could have been a retired janitor or former president of the university. But Andy remembered one particular conversation.

The old man told his story.

"When I was l7 I carved my initials into a birch tree with a little heart around them and an arrow through the heart saying that I loved EW. And I feel confident that I did love EW. However, after a passionate but short courtship, it all ended. I wanted to cut the tree down with an ax. When I was 35, I visited the tree again. I remembered the good times with EW and the tree only evoked a melancholy smile. When I was 65, I visited the tree for a third time and pondered, but my only thoughts were, 'What was EW's last name?' I suppose if I live to be 85, the tree itself may be forgotten. I also suppose that all of life's issues, from one's love affairs to the rise and fall of nations, are that way. Today's headlines will be tomorrow's lining for the floor of a bird cage. Yesterday will be misplaced somewhere in the long forgotten recesses of our mind. The only thing remaining will be the shape of the mind. Am I a bitter character because of the aborted love affair? Have I survived to love again? What is my condition now? After you have experienced it all, who are you? All of our existence is nothing more than a conversation with or about character. The conversation passes. Our character remains."

"What does it say to us?" Andy inquired.

"Hold fast to what you are and you will never be more."

Conclusion

Andy did learn some mathematics while at Chapel Hill. That was his major. Since he finished the required number of semester hours in August, the university mailed him his diploma with instructions that he could attend the graduation ceremony the following year. He never attended.

With his formal education behind him, he saluted the university for accomplishing its purpose and resumed his informal education.

He returned to work for the telephone company.

THE PRISONER

Attention to detail,
Examine to see,
A prisoner in chains,
Who yearns to be free.

An accomplished recluse,
And often ignored,
To closest friend,
Mystery's source.

Sound the retreat,
If provoked to reveal,
A turtle in shell,
With permanent seal.

Yea or nay a muffled scream,
Choosing sides a feat,
Afraid of trampling,
Vulnerable to feet.

Exposed to the world,
Countenance a mask,
Peril is its suitor,
If it attempts to laugh.

Attractive delusions,
Rose-colored paths,
Lost in confusion,
Seeking things, hell bent.

A contorted face,
For a matinee,
A truth or a lie,
As the feature dims?

Escape cried the jailer!
Solitude's our friend.
We'll there fix our gaze,
With no blink nor bend.

A PROMOTION?

Andy enjoyed his work with the telephone company. The company was growing, and because of his additional education, Andy was placed in the planning department. Hank had also returned to school to complete his college education. They worked in the same department.

It was like old times. They again played basketball for the company team, played ping-pong on breaks in the company lounge, and ate lunch together. They also planned for and installed a lot of telephone equipment around Eastern North Carolina.

And then a position in management became available. Hank and Andy stood in front of the bulletin board and read together. The bulletin stated: "NOTICE: A position as crew chief has become available in the planning department. The company has decided that the position will be filled from the ranks of existing planning department personnel. Interviews with candidates will be conducted in the near future."

Speculation throughout the department began immediately concerning who would be promoted.

Mr. Johnson called Andy into his office to discuss the promotion.

"Andy, you are on the list from which the new crew chief will be selected," Mr. Johnson said.

"Well, I'm flattered," Andy answered.

"I don't know if you should be flattered or not. The position will call for you to continue much as you are now, but you will be given the additional responsibilities of management. Ultimately, you would assume only management duties. How would you feel about being in management?"

"I honestly hadn't thought much about it. I may need some time to respond."

"Well, take a week. We'll talk again later."

"Do you mind my asking the names of others on the list?"

"No, everyone will learn anyway. The list has been reduced to just you and Hank. Your histories with the company are remarkably similar. Both came to work at the same time. Both have had advanced education. Both are very capable. It will be a hard decision. That's the main reason I called you in, just to talk, get your feelings on the matter."

"That's going to make it harder for me."

Andy arose from his chair and started to leave. As he reached the door, he turned and said, "Mr. Johnson, I wouldn't be disappointed if the company gave Hank the position."

"I have already talked to Hank. You'll probably not be surprised to learn that he said essentially the same thing," Mr. Johnson said, "but I have to choose."

Andy invited Hank to *TimeNot* for the weekend. They talked about the promotion at a leisurely pace over supper.

"They're dragging us kicking and screaming into the rat race, Andy, whether we want to go or not."

"I know what you mean. The race kind of sucks you in. I mean, I was happy just going to work and spending my weekends here at *TimeNot*."

"Not much display of ambition there, old friend."

"I probably learned that from my grandpa. He believed that if you straighten yourself out and did a good days work for a decent salary, the direction ambition takes you would take care of itself."

"I see it that way too. A job just provides you with the means to have barbecues in your back yard. A higher paying job just allows you to have bigger barbecues. In the end, when you, or maybe your caterers, have cleaned the grill, you're left with yourself."

They were quiet.

"Mr. Johnson told me that you said I could have the position," Andy said.

"And he told me the same thing about you."

"We agree then? It doesn't matter who gets the position?"

"Fine with me either way," Hank said as they closed the conversation.

They relaxed over supper.

Mr. Johnson called Andy and Hank into his office the following week.

"This was one of the hardest decision I have had to make. I thought about flipping a coin. There is virtually no difference between the two of you. I have never seen two records so nearly identical." He paused. "But there was one difference which would ordinarily be negligible. As I have already said, there are no real differences."

He turned to Hank and said "Hank, you came to work one day after Andy. If I remember correctly, your dad was sick. Based on nothing more than one day's seniority, Andy gets the job."

Hank reached over to Andy and offered his hand. It was not a congratulatory offer, but one confirming the conversation they had had at *TimeNot*.

"From what you two have said earlier, there will be no problem."

"Certainly not," Hank said.

"My struggling to choose may be rendered moot within six months. The company is adding another crew within that time. That crew chief position will certainly be yours, Hank."

"Thank you, Mr. Johnson," Hank said.

"I'm sure you'll do a good job, Andy," said Mr. Johnson, offering his hand.

Mr. Johnson was accurate in his evaluation of the situation on three counts. Andy continued to work as hard as he had before but with management duties. The promotion affected Hank and Andy's friendship not at all. Hank made crew chief six months later.

MIDNIGHT

Treasures in pits,
Enticingly,
Blinded by Midnight,
Dark Midnight and me.

Illusions so bright,
Foolishly,
Reaching for Midnight,
For Midnight to see.

Pinnacles without seats,
Restlessly,
Trusting in Midnight,
In Midnight to be.

Emily attended college at East Carolina in Greenville because it was convenient. She earned a Bachelor of Arts Degree in Education with a minor in music. She stayed home with her family while doing so. Upon graduation she went to work for a local bank, moved into an apartment of her own, and settled into a routine. She often called it a rut. She sang in church. She sang at her friends' weddings. She wondered if she would ever have a wedding of her own. She visited her mother early one Saturday night.

"Mom, Joseph and I ended it all tonight. We broke up."

"Well, I'm sorry to hear that," her mother said. "He was such a nice boy. I thought you two were getting along just fine."

"We were. And he really was, Mom. Things just didn't work out."

Emily placed her head on her mom's shoulder and cried.

Her mom waited.

"Anyway, it lasted five months," Emily finally said. She shrugged her shoulders and plopped down on the couch. Her mom sat down beside her.

"If it's going to make you feel this way, why did you break up?"

"I don't think I was really crying over Joseph, Mom. We have both known for weeks now that it wasn't going to work out. We just hesitated to call it quits."

Emily thought about it.

"I think I was just crying because the promise didn't work out."

"Well then, I reckon it's all for the best. Some people don't find out it's not going to work until there's a lot more pain involved in breaking up."

"I know. I'm glad I found out now instead of later. I'm also glad I have a mom like you to complain to."

They hugged each other.

"You know you're still my little baby. Come complain to me any time."

"Little baby! I'm 25 years old."

"You'll always be my little baby."

She patted Emily on the knee.

"And besides being the best mother in the whole world, you're my only confidante. What would I do without you?"

"Any time, sweetheart. Any time."

They paused.

"I expect you haven't eaten. Would you like a little snack?"

"Not only can you read my mind, you can read my stomach too."

They went into the kitchen and had a sandwich together.

"I guess I'll just stay in this same old rut," Emily said, continuing to unload on her mother. "I feel like an airplane in a holding pattern over the airport. Around and around and around." Emily paused and then continued. "I went to McDonald's restaurant the other day and before I could say anything, the attendant asked if I wanted my usual sausage and egg biscuit. My predictability annoyed me so much I said no out of frustration. I then ordered an egg and sausage biscuit."

They both laughed.

"I certainly agree with you, Sweetheart. Life can get a little too routine."

"What do you do to avoid being so routine?"

"Take up a new project. Visit an old friend. Visit a new church."

"I've tried those. I still feel I'm in a holding pattern."

"Well, for starters, let's drive up to Raleigh tomorrow and see your Aunt Janie. We could even do a little shopping."

"That sounds good," Emily answered.

They continued their conversation until late into the night. Emily thought how blessed she was to have such a mother.

Emily's mom finally said, "You might as well spend the night. You know your room is just like you left it."

Emily did spend the night. She enjoyed the feel of her old bed. Her own apartment was nice but so was home. She curled up under the covers and remembered her childhood days.

She thought of Joseph and again felt the disappointment.

She finally succeeded in directing her thoughts to the future. Was there someone there for her? She doubted. She anticipated. She hoped.

A VISITOR

Andy enjoyed working and appreciated the conveniences of his apartment in Jacksonville, but his heart was always toward *TimeNot*. He returned every chance he got.

On this particular day *TimeNot* was quiet as usual. Andy was eating his favorite breakfast of sausage and eggs cooked over the open fire.

"Ditto, do you hear a car coming?" Andy asked as he gave Ditto his share of the sausage.

Andy listened.

A car finally exited the cart path into *TimeNot*. It was a Cadillac.

"Who could this be, Ditto? I don't know many people who own a Cadillac."

Andy set his plate on the table and arose from his chair to greet his mystery visitor.

A rather distinguished appearing lady got out of the car. Her graying hair was fixed nicely on top of her head. Andy guessed her age to be between 45 and 50. She wore a suit and high heels.

"You must be Andy," she said as she approached. "Your neighbors have told me what a fine fellow you are."

Ditto greeted her with a friendly wag of his tail.

"Yes, but I don't have the slightest idea who you are," Andy answered.

"Well, I came to this place before you were born. It was many years ago. I knew Alvin very well," she said wistfully.

Andy began to suspect he knew her identity.

"We were very close," she continued as she slowly looked around. She finally shook her head back and forth and closed her eyes.

Andy watched her stand motionless for quite some time. He said, "You must be Kathleen."

"How did you know?"

"I heard Alvin mention you on one occasion. Sitting right here by this fire."

"So he mentioned me just once, did he?"

"Yes, you probably know how Alvin was. But, I could tell you were something special."

Andy waited for Kathleen to collect her thoughts.

"There was a time when we were special to each other. Before he went off to war." Her voice became almost inaudible.

Andy could see that it was time to listen. He motioned for Kathleen to sit down.

"I would like to hear about it."

"Thank you," she said and took a seat.

Andy was obviously sympathetic, and she continued.

"We were sweethearts. No one lived here at the time." She continued her trip down memory lane. "We would steal away to this place to be together. We swam in the river."

Andy's attentive silence encouraged her to continue.

"I loved him and he loved me."

She selected each word carefully.

"I still loved him when he came home from the war with his injuries."

She was selective again.

"You know, I didn't demand or need perfection. Love does not do that. Just total dedication to love would have been enough. Imperfections would have taken care of themselves."

While she reminisced, Andy did some visualizing. He could see Kathleen and Alvin as youngsters frolicking in the seclusion of *TimeNot*. He could see young love in full bloom.

"But he couldn't accept his imperfections caused by his injuries. They really didn't matter to me. I would have stayed right here in this place with him forever. I told him so."

Andy continued to listen.

"But.... He literally ran me away."

Tears filled her eyes.

Andy retrieved a paper towel and offered it to Kathleen. He held onto her hand as he gave it to her. For a moment they shared the hurt. Her burden seemed lighter with Andy helping.

"I'll be all right," she said as she took the towel and wiped the tears away.

"Cleansing tears are not only welcomed at *TimeNot*, they are encouraged." Andy smiled.

"You are wise beyond your years, Andy. And I might add, kind."

"*TimeNot* has a way of encouraging such things."

Andy paused.

"He's buried right over yonder," Andy pointed.

Kathleen gazed in the grave's direction. She returned to her car, pulled off her coat and shoes, pulled her blouse loose from her skirt, and began to walk toward the grave.

"I haven't been barefooted in ages. Want to come with me?"

"I'll wait here." Andy decided to leave her alone with her thoughts. He continued his breakfast and glanced in her direction ever so often. She sat by the grave for 30 minutes. Andy finished breakfast and washed his dishes. He waited.

"Want some breakfast?" he asked as she returned.

"I ate at the motel before I came here, but that sausage and egg you were eating looked really good."

"I'll fix you a sandwich."

Andy began cooking.

"You're staying at a motel?"

"Yes, I'm in town for my 30th high school reunion."

"What you been doing all these years?"

"I'm a fashion designer. I've traveled most of the world, but I think, if I could, I'd trade it all for just this little spot right here. I've decided that success is a distraction."

Kathleen ate her sandwich. They exchanged stories about Alvin. Andy told her about himself. It was a most pleasant and revealing meeting which stretched well into the afternoon.

Kathleen reluctantly said, "I must be going, Andy. It has been an absolute pleasure."

"You are welcome anytime. And we will not be distracted."

"No, this has always been a beautiful place to get away to."

"But wait, I almost forgot. I have something for you."

Andy went over to the hiding place in the brick grate and removed three bricks.

Kathleen was puzzled as she followed.

Andy reached in and, after setting aside several jars of money, retrieved the bundle of unopened letters Kathleen had written to Alvin 30 years before.

"Aren't you afraid someone will steal your money?" Kathleen asked while still wondering about Andy's actions.

"There are no such beasts in *TimeNot*," Andy smiled and said as he handed the bundle of letters to Kathleen.

Kathleen was amazed as she shuffled through the letters.

She said regretfully, "Unopened."

She pined, "But he did keep them."

She tried to recall the contents. "It may hurt too much to read these."

An aching filled her bosom. She hugged Andy.

"Thank you, Andy."

She clutched the letters to her breast and returned to her car to drive away.

THE MEETING

A mutual sighting,
Demanding advance.
Ageless attractions,
Relentlessly pull.

Reciprocating glances,
Alluring retreats,
Wistful flirtations,
A jousting, a game.

With fun to be had,
The advances made,
A nagging doubt,
Sincere or whim?

All wondering ended,
Betrayed by smiles.
One half each,
Now a radiant whole.

A pit, a void,
A moment ago.
A boundless horizon,
Begins to unfold.

THE MEETING

Andy walked the well-worn path along the river at the state park in Goldsboro. It was early morning. Visitors had not yet begun their trek to the park. Park rangers were about. The path was lined with blooming azaleas. Bees and hummingbirds visited the blossoms. A bend in the river, just ahead, was a portion of the river which opened into a small meadow. It made a horseshoe curve through the meadow. Daffodils, Easter lilies, buttercups, and the ever-present dandelions filled the meadow. The dandelions were in some ways the prettiest with their staunchly independent crowns waving in the breeze.

There were sandy shores along the river. Come summer, the swimmers would appear and sunbathers would cover the shores. Before this day was finished, the meadow would be flooded, not with water, but with humanity. This early in the morning, however, he was alone, or so he thought.

He meandered along the path, looking, smelling, listening, feeling.

It was the kind of day when butterflies would rest unafraid on an offered palm. And he offered. It was the kind of day when the warm breezes would, if you listened intensely, whisper the secrets of their travels to far away places. And he listened. It was the kind of day when the smell of the flowers was intoxicating. And he smelled. It was the kind of day which made one believe in a place where frogs really do become kings. And he believed.

These were the first few warm days of spring.

When he reached the opening to the meadow, he stood for ten minutes, absorbing the sensations, before continuing his walk. In the distance, at the other end of the meadow, he saw someone coming. He could not determine if the person was male or female. He had no way of knowing that the person was Emily.

If they continued in their present directions, they would meet along the sandy river shore. He would not change directions. Someone so solitary this early in the morning would surely be interesting.

When he was close enough to determine that the person was female, his mind began racing, searching for words to sound clever, words to introduce himself, words which would invite, words which would not scare her away.

His reluctance to speak came to his rescue. He said nothing.

As they were just a few feet apart, he looked into her eyes for a moment and she into his.

Her eyes were deep. They were windows through which he could envision delicious mysteries.

Wrestling with her shyness, Emily at first looked away. But his face had been friendly. She returned his glance.

They smiled.

He bowed his head indicating a hello. He still said nothing.

She did the same.

They had been slowly walking toward each other and they were now almost alongside. Andy then held up one finger indicating, "One moment, please".

She stopped.

He then ran down closer to the river's edge where the sand was smooth and began drawing.

She watched.

He drew in the sand a carriage with big wheels and one seat in the middle pulled by four horses. He backed away from his drawing and turned to Emily with a sweeping bow and a wave of an imaginary hat, inviting her aboard.

With Andy still bowing, Emily walked closer to see his drawing.

She smiled.

He opened the 'door'.

She paused, and then stepped in, leaning on Andy's offered hand.

He followed, closed the 'door', and took his place beside her. Andy started the 'horses' with a crack of his 'whip'.

They 'rode' along at a leisurely pace. Emily would point at a flower. Andy would look. Andy would point and Emily would look. Smiles were plentiful.

Neither had said anything, giving the other's imagination a chance to fill in the blanks. Their imaginations were working overtime. Anticipation sharpened their senses. They liked each other. Body language, glances, smiles, and gentle gestures conveyed feelings which could not be expressed with the spoken word.

Was time moving at all? They were now oblivious to everything but each other. Common sense suggested caution, but each was willing to suspend common sense for the sake of this enthralling, nonsensical, mystical, wonderful experience. Each was beginning to feel this relationship was unique.

Andy looked at Emily and said boldly, "I am Andrew. I am your knight in shining armor. I have come to rescue you".

More smiles.

Emily digested his words and responded, "I am Emily. We shall see if you are my knight in shining armor."

Andy discarded his airs and said plainly, "When I shed my nobility, people just call me Andy."

They knew names. Both anticipated more.

As they came to a park bench, Andy pulled back on the 'reins' saying, "Whooooooa." The 'horses' stopped. He dismounted, opened the 'door,' and held out his hand for Emily's support so that she might follow. They walked over to the park bench and sat down.

"Tell Andy about Emily, from here, not here," he said as he lightly beat first on his chest and then pointed to his head.

The form of his request and gestures suggested that he and Emily would examine Emily with sheer unadulterated, exuberant interest.

She took him at his word.

"Emily is 26 years old. She attended East Carolina in Greenville. She is a bank vice president at a small branch bank in Greenville. That's another word for loan officer."

She liked the feeling of talking about herself in the third person. It gave her a new perspective with clarity of thought. But mostly she enjoyed telling Andy, who was totally devoted to listening. His chin was in his hand as his arm was propped on the back of the bench. He leaned toward Emily and did not, indeed he could not, take his eyes off her. He hardly moved except for a nod of his head to encourage her.

She was encouraged and continued.

"Emily has lived in Greenville all her life. She has her own apartment, but close to her parents. She has one brother and the family is close."

She paused. She was seeking encouragement.

Andy nodded and pointed to his bosom, indicating an interest in her feelings.

She understood. She felt a warm rush inside as if he had touched her with his finger instead of his own bosom. She felt as if a computer-like, down-load function had been pushed within. She eagerly picked up her pace.

"Emily loves blue because it's soft and serene, like water."

She paused briefly.

He nodded approvingly.

"Her favorite number is seven, not because it's lucky, but because in the Bible it represents wholeness, completeness, closure, an end to contending. She had rather agree than argue even if pride is the loser."

She was surprised at her revelations about herself. She waited.

He nodded and gave her an enthusiastic 'thumbs-up' signal.

A growing trust told her she could continue.

"She has always been shy, at least before today," confessing she usually didn't talk this much. "She has had to struggle with the associated problems of shyness - nervous in a crowd, etc."

Reaching into the deepest recesses of her soul, she said, "Love is the only thing that matters - all the rest is by-the-way."

She felt drained, she felt exposed, she felt naked. She had never before said such things to anybody in such a manner. How would he respond? She decided that if he responded with anything resembling a laugh, she would run away as hard as she could. She turned to look at him.

Andy looked at Emily.

Emily could see tears in his eyes.

Such honesty astounded him. Even though he had asked, he didn't expect such an answer. He knew she was vulnerable, and his response was ever so important. He took his arm from the back of the bench, leaned forward, put his elbows on his knees with his chin in both hands and hesitated. He was thankful. He was full. Was this the priceless treasure which sat next to him?

Emily watched anxiously, hopefully.

Andy finally turned to Emily with a burst of inspiration. He held up his one finger indicating again, "Just a moment". He jumped up, ran down to the water's edge, reached upward with open hands unto the sky, and almost yelled, "Yes!" He was excited. And then one more time, but somewhat subdued, "Yes." He was satisfied. And one final time with one outstretched arm and open hand toward Emily, "Yes." He approved.

Emily's fears vanished. She was not alone with her thoughts in an impregnable fortress. The rescue had begun.

He looked at Emily.

Emily returned his gaze.

He savored the moment.

Andy came back and sat down beside Emily with his legs and feet stretched out in front, his head in clasped hands behind his head. He was at peace with the world.

Emily joined him in his pose.

They savored the moment together.

THE FLOWER

A trek through the desert,
Straining to see,

Nestled in thorns,
Of the cactus tree,

Its flower, so barren,
By two set free.

THE MEETING - ANDY'S TURN

Andy closed his eyes and began daydreaming. The beautiful spring day all but vanished. Birds were not heard. Water did not flow. Flowers did not smell. Time did not move.

Emily looked at Andy as he was daydreaming.

Lost in his thoughts of Emily, he was oblivious to everything, even Emily. He had again forgotten that he was a participant in the ongoing drama.

Emily looked at Andy's nose.

His mind's eye had taken control. He could now see an endless yellow brick road with just him and Emily, hand-in-hand, its only travelers. They were enough.

Emily looked at Andy's hair.

It suddenly occurred to Andy that in his daydreaming, he had, although inspired by her, left Emily behind. He would return for her. He would see if Emily was feeling any such wonder. He glanced her way only to see her looking at him.

She satisfied his wondering glance.

"I have been there."

Although she did not know where 'there' was she could see that he was 'traveling'.

"I have been there too, but before, I was alone."

He allowed her to conclude that she was with him.

"Tell Emily about Andy, from here," indicating to her chest as Andy had done but neglecting to point at the head. It was no longer necessary to indicate that only heart-to-heart conversation was preferred.

Emily had been honestly revealing. He would do the same.

"Andy's obviously a dreamer," explaining his 'trip' and pausing to collect his thoughts.

He searched his soul, believing he could trust Emily.

"But he tries to not make dreaming his master," paraphrasing Rudyard Kipling. "He does not always succeed."

Andy took a deep breath.

"He admits an almost irrational hope in triumphant good."

He paused.

"He believes there is a place where dreaming is the norm, where hurting is nonexistent, where disappointment is yesterday. It is an island of serene calm in a disorderly world."

He paused.

"He believes that love makes all of this possible. Love never fails."

He paused again and allowed Emily time to consider what he had said. He waited for her approval.

She said softly, almost breathlessly, "Go ahead."

"Sad to say, this place is itself not the norm. Hard work is an absolutely necessary ingredient."

Another pause.

"Love is not something you turn over a rock and find. You cannot reach down and pick up a handful. You must seize it with your heart. You must submit to it with your heart. You must nurture it and cherish its existence more than your life or even the life of anyone who would share such a place."

He allowed Emily more time to consider.

"Love is as much a looking outward together as far as you can, and seeing the same star, as it is being spellbound or enchanted with another person."

He waited for Emily to absorb his words.

"Love is akin to fantasy, make-believe, if you will. But if just two people believe, it is no longer make-believe. They may build such a world. He strives to be such person and searches for one more such person."

He was quiet. He was pleasantly exhausted. He was the one who was now vulnerable.

Tears filled Emily's eyes. What should she do?

She simply moved closer and placed her head on Andy's shoulder.

Andy leaned over and placed his head on top of Emily's.

They sat together. They were totally immersed in wonderful thoughts of someone who may be, and from all appearances was, an answer to longings solitarily endured for a lifetime.

They believed.

Andy gently broke the wonderful silence.

"Does Emily want Andy's particulars, his non-vital statistics?"

Emily realized she knew nothing of Andy's station in life while at the same time feeling that she had known him forever. And here she was with her head on his shoulder. Never before had she acquainted herself with someone heart first. With the foundation they had just laid, anything subsequently constructed would stand. She was satisfied the 'by-the-way' material would not crumble this relationship.

"Let me guess," she said playfully. "He's J. Paul Getty's grandson with zillions of dollars in his bank account."

"No."

"He really is royalty from England with zillions of dollars in his bank account."

"No."

"He's a penniless bum who has never worked a day in his life."

"No."

Emily said seriously, "I believe nothing you say can or will disappoint me".

Andy began, "Andy lives in Jacksonville and works for the telephone company in planning. If the telephone company expands or changes, Andy plans. His family is remarkably ordinary. Andy loves blue for the same reasons you gave. Seven is now his favorite number. Andy loves to play tennis, basketball, etceteras. You name it."

"Totally acceptable," said Emily. "Tennis on the l2th of next month at ten in Greenville?" Emily questioned.

"It's a date, and a date, and a date, and so on," Andy beamed.

The future was suddenly bursting at its seams.

When their joy had subsided, Andy said, "Of a more immediate concern is lunch. I'll buy."

"I'll eat," said Emily.

And off they went.

Their 'carriage' had become a cloud. The future was now.

THE FOUR-HOUR SANDWICH

Andy and Emily rode to Goldsboro, leaving Emily's car at the park.

"Any place in particular you'd like to eat?" Andy asked.

"Nope, they can serve raw slugs for all I care," Emily said, indicating her contentment.

"Raw slugs it is," Andy smiled.

"Maybe you could find a place with a bacon and egg sandwich as backup. Just in case they run out of slugs." Emily smiled.

They found a restaurant.

"Got any raw slugs?" Andy asked the waitress jovially. "We're really hungry this morning."

"Don't pay any attention to him. We're both a little giddy right now," Emily joined in while laughing.

"It doesn't take a rocket scientist to see that. But I don't have time for your foolishness." The waitress smiled. She then mustered all the authority she could in her voice and said, "Give me your order."

"Two bacon and egg sandwiches with coffee," Andy ordered with raised shoulders, palms up, and questioning eyes toward Emily.

"Perfect."

The waitress left.

"So I'm giddy, am I?" Andy asked.

"I couldn't find a better word if I had a thesaurus."

"Well, I'd say you're giddy. I'm collected, composed."

"Oh sure. And who's ordering slugs?"

They laughed heartily.

When the laughter had subsided, Andy looked into Emily's eyes, reached to take her hands in his, and said, "Emily, if this is giddy then let me be giddy forever."

"I know," Emily responded.

They might have gazed at each other forever, but the waitress brought their coffee.

"Have I got to pry you two apart?" The waitress asked as she poured the coffee. "How long have you known each other anyway?"

"Oh, since about 9:30 this morning or forever. I'm not quite sure," Emily said.

"Oh, boy. Well, be careful, Honey. He's a member of the opposite sex. Can't always trust them, you know."

"Don't the two of you gang up on me now," Andy said.

"I'll take my chances," Emily said.

"Anyway," Andy said repeating a joke he had heard recently, "no one's ever going to win the battle of the sexes. Too much fraternizing with the enemy."

And so it went. If Emily opted for the road to absurdity, Andy followed. If Andy went searching for 'serious', Emily followed. Any road, or cloud, or magic carpet would do. They were together.

"The weaker sex?" Emily cried. "I'm as strong as any man."

"Oh, yeah," Andy responded. "Put her there," he said as he placed his elbow on the table with hand in the air.

They arm wrestled. Andy saw to it that no one won. He did not want to win. Had Emily not thereby won?

"Sweet ties brawn," Andy conceded as they both gave up.

"A tie suits me just fine," Emily said. "Why would I want to get the better of myself?"

And they again looked into each other's eyes.

And the conversation continued.

"You know we're trying to catch lightning in a bottle, Emily," Andy said softly.

"I know that, Andy. You hold the bottle. I'll turn the cap real tight."

And the conversation continued.

"Do you think we ought to go?" Andy suggested.

"Why would I want to go? I'm already there," Emily responded.

And they talked.

"I don't even know your address or telephone number," said Andy.

They exchanged addresses and telephone numbers.

And they talked on.

"What did you think of the '60's? Did you do any protesting?" Emily queried.

"They certainly were some violent times. The hippies, the flower children, they asked some good questions. 'Where have all the flowers gone? Where have all the graveyards gone? How many roads must a man walk down? How many cannon balls must fly? Is this the eve of destruction?' Those are questions we have all wondered about, and I have certainly asked myself. If they had offered an answer, I think I would have joined them. They didn't and I didn't."

"What's your answer, Andy?"

"I'm hoping that a big part of my own personal answer is sitting across this table from me."

They shared another smile. Modesty between them had disappeared since Emily first looked away and then looked into Andy's eyes at the river. They were comfortable with each other.

"The answer for humanity may be more complicated."

Andy thought a little. Emily waited.

"Or maybe not, Emily. Do you think it's possible for humanity to feel towards each other as lovers feel?"

"That certainly would solve the world's problems. Make love, not war."

"So, you're suggesting my answer is the same as the hippies'."

"No. I'm sure you mean 'love' to be more than sexual intercourse with anyone who comes along or sharing the same needle."

"Yes! I couldn't have said it better myself. And I'm still working on the correct definition for love."

"I'll help."

They rested. They waited to see where either of them might want to direct the conversation. Each knew it could be anywhere. There would be no topics 'off limits' for them.

They talked of their college years, growing up, brothers and sisters, and Vietnam. Emily cried when she heard about Bob.

The waitress came by. "You know this booth is cheaper by the week."

"We'll take it," Andy said.

"I'm not trying to run you off, understand. But don't you two have somewhere to go?"

They looked at each other.

"Nope," Emily finally offered.

"You can bring us a Coke though. Coffee is growing old," Andy said.

And they talked on.

"You know what's always bugged me about this world?" Andy started.

"What?" Emily said excitedly and sat up on the edge of her seat.

Emily's enthusiasm was catching, and Andy launched into the subject without his usual delay.

"There's no place you can drive a stake and be sure it will be there tomorrow."

"What do you mean?"

"Well, everything changes. I have seen mighty oak trees pushed over by bulldozers. Ideas come and go. Friends and enemies alike pass away. There's no solid ground."

"I'll be your stake," Emily said again, displaying her enthusiasm.

"You knew I wanted to hear that, didn't you?"

"Yes."

"And I'll be yours."

"Yes."

They had skipped a few questions and answers with their quick responses and the conversation never skipped a beat. Were they already so close that they could read the other's mind?

Andy put on a most serious face.

"I'll tell you something else this world needs."

"What's that?"

He could see that he had Emily's complete attention.

"A good five-cent bar of soap with a hole in the middle so that little piece won't always be left over."

Emily reached over and gave Andy a little pinch.

They laughed.

He held her hand.

In the late afternoon Andy said, "We'd better go get your car. The park will be closed."

"You're right. I had almost forgotten it."

Andy took a ten-dollar bill from his pocket and gave it to the waitress.

"Don't tell me you leaving. You've become a fixture around here," she said.

"We're finally out of your way," Andy said.

"You certainly have not been in the way. It has been a delight watching. It even brings back a few memories," she said wistfully.

She returned with Andy's change, leaned over to Emily, and said in a hushed tone loud enough for Andy to hear, "I couldn't help watching and hearing some of your conversation, and you might ought to consider keeping this one."

"I'm considering it real hard," Emily whispered back.

"I heard that," Andy said as he stood up. As the waitress laid the change on the table, Andy took her hand in his, leaned over, and gave it a kiss. "If I were not occupied this evening, I'd ask you out myself."

"Oh, get out of here."

The ride back to the park was quiet. Both pondered the wonderful day. They were aglow in each other's presence. Emily considered sliding closer to Andy. She even thought about placing her arm around his shoulders. But there was no rush. Just how long was forever, she wondered.

Andy pulled his car alongside Emily's. They stood by her door facing each other.

Andy began slowly.

"Emily."

He was not calling her. He was just repeating her name.

"Emily," he said again. "I cannot tell you how much I have enjoyed this day."

He paused for breath.

"But I'm going to try."

He backed away a little to give himself room to motion with his arms.

"If I could have taken a catalog and ordered a day, it would have been this day."

He spread his arms, indicating that the day encompassed all that had happened.

"It would have begun at about 9:30. The breezes, the aroma would have been just so. I would have seen a girl in the distance."

He paused.

"She would come gently forward and take her place in my senses. I would feel at once nonsensical and sober, elated and calm, boundless and contained. But most of all I would be contented in her presence."

He looked at Emily.

"Her eyes would sparkle. They would be windows to a soul as soft as a sigh."

He paused.

"Her name would be Emily."

Andy's hands were now clasped behind his back. He leaned forward and kissed Emily ever so lightly on her lips. They barely touched. He placed his cheek against Emily's and whispered her name in her ear. He backed away and opened his eyes to see Emily motionless before him. Her eyes were still closed and her head tilted toward him.

"Andrew," she whispered.

She opened her eyes and leaned back against her car.

"Andy, that was intoxicating."

"I know."

Andy opened Emily's door.

As she drove away, Andy called after her, "I'll call tonight."

Emily waved.

They both returned to their apartments, Emily in Greenville, Andy in Jacksonville. When Emily was ready for bed, her phone rang. She knew it was Andy.

"I'm just making sure I didn't dream it all," Andy said.

"I know," Emily responded.

"Did I really meet a girl in Goldsboro today?"

"Yes, you did."

They reviewed the day. It was beautiful all over again. When they hung up their phones, neither was alone. The other's presence remained very real.

Andy called again. "You know, Emily. The number of people you're surrounded by notwithstanding, you're really alone in this world until someone says 'I understand'."

"I understand, Andy."

Dreams would be sweet in Greenville tonight.

Dreams would be sweet in Jacksonville tonight.

EPIPHANY
(Andy Dreams)

She came as a summer breeze,
Refreshing,
Her presence an end,
The beast at rest.

He wanted no more,
Appetites waned,
Existence divine,
A Shangri La with hand in hand.

Searching had ended,
Time very still,
A moment eternal,
Contentment supreme.

And then he noticed with utter delight,
That his love had breasts.
And a longing forgotten in the sublime,
Would also find its promised niche.

The twain together,
A mirror reflection,
Inseparably entwined ---
But only an epiphany.

EPIPHANY
(Emily Dreams)

He came as a gentle force,
Strong.
His presence an end,
The beast at rest.

She wanted no more,
Appetites waned,
Existence divine,
A Shangri La with hand in hand.

Searching had ended,
Time very still,
A moment eternal,
Contentment supreme.

And then she thought with utter delight,
She could, with bosom emptied,
Taking aught but love, a like exchange,
Give unto him her only gift.

The twain together,
A mirror reflection,
Inseparably entwined ---
But only an epiphany.

GETTING TO KNOW YOU

Bright and early the next morning, Andy was knocking on Emily's door. Emily was waiting. They spent the day together. They spent many days together. There were phone calls between Greenville and Jacksonville. Andy and Emily came to refer to the phone calls as 'Touching You'. They experienced spontaneous smiles at work, remembering something funny or pleasant the other had said over the weekend. A 'Touching You' phone call would follow. They played tennis on the l2th as promised. Tennis became a regular thing. Andy met Mr. and Mrs. Wheeler. Mr. Wheeler cooked hamburgers and hot dogs over a charcoal fire in the back yard. Mrs. Wheeler took great pleasure in reminding Emily that she had told her she would find a boy worth the wait. Emily agreed.

"Emily," Andy said on one of the phone calls, "I have some place I'd like for us to go this weekend."

"Where?" Emily was her normally eager self.

"Well, I have this retreat. Very private. Very secluded. Some have called it desolate."

"Sounds interesting. Tell me more."

"But it is definitely not desolate. If anything, it is a place where one may find unexpected treasures."

"Keep going."

"You'll need something to swim in."

"It has a place to swim?"

"Oh, yes. And I think I can safely say that you will not believe the conveniences. A nice, solid, little privy. I leveled it myself.

Fresh, cool, hand-pumped water from an underground flow." Andy paused. "You'll just have to see it to believe it."

"I'm ready, Andy. As long as you're going to be there."

"Nobody but me and you. I'll see you first thing in the morning. We can spend Saturday, Saturday night, and Sunday there."

They arrived at *TimeNot* Saturday morning. Andy got out of the car and unlocked the gate.

Emily noted Andy's board with *TimeNot* burned into it.

Neither said a word as they drove down the bumpy cart path. The summer growth of bushes along the path brushed the car on both sides. They looked at each other several times as they negotiated the path. Andy said nothing but was examining Emily to see her reactions. She just smiled back. They parked the car in front of the old house, got out, and stood by the car.

Andy waited for Emily to look around.

The goats had discovered their presence and came running. They were suddenly surrounded by ten goats including two which were four weeks old.

"Well, look at that, Andy. Are they yours?"

"Oh, yes. It's all mine."

Andy retrieved some ears of corn from a bag hanging under the pump shelter, and they fed the goats from their hands. Emily patted the kids. They then threw some corn on the ground so the goats would leave them alone.

Emily continued her exploration of the place. She walked down by the river with Andy following.

"Swimming as advertised," Andy smiled.

Emily feigned disbelief.

They walked by the privy.

"Conveniences as advertised," Andy smiled again as he opened the door to display the inside. "Clean, don't you think? I came out here yesterday just to clean everything."

"I've only seen pictures of these things in a book," Emily said, appearing disbelieving again.

They walked through the old barnyard. The bantam chickens gathered around as Andy threw corn to them. A hen had seven biddies. Emily tried to draw near, but the chickens stayed just out of reach.

They returned to the front of the house and Emily fixed her eyes on the board nailed to the porch post with *TimeNot* burned into it. She turned to Andy with a quizzical expression.

"That's the name of my retreat."

"What does it mean?"

Andy did not respond quickly.

Emily had become accustomed to Andy's pace, but he was taking longer than usual to answer. She did not ask again, but waited, knowing that he would respond.

Andy sat down on the edge of the porch and motioned for Emily to sit beside him.

She did.

"The simple answer I give most people when they ask is that time, or at least its passing, does not much matter around here. And that's true, but it is much more than that."

He paused.

"Emily, time speaks clearly here, and there are some things only time can say. 'No.' 'Yes.' It does not repeat itself. It says whatever just once and waits for you to understand. Time says to the raging bull, 'Be quiet'. And he is quiet. It says to the child, 'Grow'. And he grows. It says to the simple, 'Be wise'. And, if attentive, he is wise. It demands your attention like no amount of shouting can ever do."

He paused.

"I have spent a good portion of my life trying to adapt my pace and life style to accommodate the world. It turns out that I was headed in the wrong direction. My grandpa said it this way. He said that he was a moonbeam man in a hundred-thousand-watt world. Moonbeamers have it right."

Andy paused.

"Only time can measure the value of a thing. Time is a simmering pot which boils away all but the substance of a thing. You may feel time simmering at *TimeNot*. It simmers so slowly, so quietly, you can hear its message. You may discover substance. Time does not boil at *TimeNot*. Time itself may become meaningless."

Andy paused.

"Don't stop now," Emily encouraged.

"I talk with rabbits here," Andy changed modes with a smile.

Emily waited. She ignored his change, knowing that Andy's conversations were usually directed.

"Talking rabbits don't startle you?"

"Andy, if you say rabbits talk here, I'll believe it."

"There is no one to compare with my Emily," Andy said.

And he hugged her.

"I'm only a half, Andy. Together we are one."

He hugged her again and kissed her on the cheek.

They smiled.

"Now tell me about this talking rabbit."

"Well, once upon a time, I spent a couple of weeks here. As part of my daily routine I would jog down the cart path to the paved road late in the day. On the first day, I came upon a rabbit eating grass along the cart path. He was startled and ran off into the underbrush. The same thing happened the next day. But on the third day, he ran off a short distance and turned to watch me. On the fourth day, I slowed to a walk, and he ran off a shorter distance. At the end of the two-week period, I would pass within a few feet of the rabbit, and he would do little more than lift his head to look my way. I suppose if I had taken more time, I could have finally patted the rabbit. Now, I hope this does not disappoint you, but not a word was spoken. But, a conversation did occur as surely as if words were exchanged. It went something like this. Rabbit: 'I'm afraid of you.' Me: 'No need to be afraid of me; I'm just jogging. You can trust me. I mean you no harm.' Rabbit: 'Well, I do believe you. I'll just keep eating.' Only time can make such a 'conversation' possible. Those conversations are the best kind."

Andy paused again.

"Emily, I can lock the gate at the road and keep out the indifferent, the angry, the violent. I can allow only trusted friends inside, those who care."

Emily waited.

Andy knew he had Emily's complete attention and that always encouraged him.

"When I am hurt, or alone, or bruised, resilience finds its genesis here. I can cry cleansing tears and not be afraid of further hurt."

Emily waited.

"I can sit down by the river over there, and, if the wind is not blowing and the water is not flowing too swiftly, I can see my reflection. If I have a blemish on my face, I see it. The water reflects exactly what it sees. This place is like that. It is quiet. I can see myself as I am - if I do not blink."

Emily waited.

"The wind rustles the leaves but is not seen. Here I get to know the rustler of hearts."

Emily waited.

"Leaving brings a longing to return. I sometimes think that permanent abode is necessary to enjoy what *TimeNot* has to offer. A visit elsewhere contaminates and makes returning difficult."

Emily waited.

"You, Emily Wheeler, are not only a welcomed, trusted friend, you are my beloved."

And he kissed her.

Emily placed her head on Andy's shoulder.

"Oh, Andy. I liked it before you described it. Now it's absolutely beautiful to me."

"Is two a beautiful number or what?" Andy asked excitedly but not expecting an answer. "Don't you think we can fly?"

"Oh, yes. We can fly," Emily agreed.

TimeNot Visit Continues

Andy and Emily began removing from the car their suitcases and the things they had brought for the weekend. Before they finished, Ditto arrived.

Emily saw Ditto coming down the cart path.

"Look, Andy. A little dog."

"That's no dog. That's Ditto. He's half human."

"You know him?"

"Yes, he's mine too. Or maybe we belong to each other. I have to leave him with my mom and dad just up the road. He seems to know when I come to *TimeNot* and just makes his appearance. Or he might just be rambling like his dad."

Emily and Ditto became friends. Andy explained to Emily about Ditto's name and all about Doonsie.

"He'll keep the bears off us tonight," Andy said.

"Bears!" Emily responded excitedly.

"Just kidding. Just kidding."

Emily and Andy went swimming in the river. Andy explained all about Alvin and how he had inherited *TimeNot*. He showed Emily the $57,000.00. They visited Alvin's grave.

A late-day summer shower blew through with some thunder and lightning. It cooled the air. Andy and Emily watched the rain from under the pump shelter.

For supper they had sausage and eggs, cooked over the open fire and then settled down in folding, reclining chairs around the fire, hand-in-hand.

Ditto lay at their feet. The goats had settled near-by. The chickens were in their roost. They watched the day end. The rains had cleared the summer haze away, and the skies were crystal clear. Stars were well-defined points of light. The fire felt good in the cool air.

"My heart is as warm as the fire, Andy."

"That's a shower, Emily."

All was quiet.

The clouds had moved away some 75 to l00 miles. They topped out at 35,000 to 40,000 feet. Lightning bolts were visible and occurred every few seconds but were too far away for the thunder to be heard. 'Awesome' seemed inadequate to describe the sight. Emily and Andy enjoyed the heavenly fireworks. They enjoyed the evening.

All was right in their little corner of the world this night.

TRIAL BY FIRE

"Emily," Andy said on one of their Friday phone calls, "let's start the weekend off with some tennis this afternoon. I can be in Greenville by 6:30. I have my gear in the car already."

"Sounds nice. I'll be at the courts waiting."

The trip from Jacksonville to Greenville had become a familiar one for Andy. He made the trek at every opportunity. The trip's time was always shortened by anticipation. This trip, however, would be like no other.

Logging operations are common in Eastern North Carolina. A loaded truck approached the Greenville main road. The driver panicked when he pumped his brakes, and the truck did not slow down. He tried to use his gears but only succeeded in slowing the vehicle to 35 miles per hour. There was nothing more he could do but blow his horn and drive through the intersection. When he saw Andy's vehicle, he made an effort to turn to his right. The truck tractor began to tilt as the heavy logs on the trailer pushed the tractor forward in a jack-knife position. The sideways tractor collided with the left rear portion of Andy's vehicle, driving it into the ditch along the road. A vehicle coming from Andy's opposite direction collided with the trailer. The trailer then spilled its logs, and they came to rest on Andy's vehicle.

"I can see him in there," said a passerby as he peered through the twisted metal and logs at Andy's vehicle. "He's not moving."

"We've got to get these logs off this car," said a second passerby. "The car might catch on fire."

Smoke and steam appeared from under the hood of Andy's car.

They tried manually to move the logs. The logs were simply too heavy. A hunter arrived with a winch on the front bumper of his vehicle. One by one the good Samaritans slowly pulled the logs from Andy's vehicle. They were finally able to pry open Andy's door and pull him out. They laid his limp body on a blanket on the shoulder of the road and covered him with another.

Emergency personnel arrived and examined Andy.

"All of his extremities are intact. No apparent injuries except for this three-inch gash on the left side of his head. It runs from near his left eyebrow through the hair line," one said. "All of this blood and it didn't even get on his shirt."

"His vitals are all stable. That's remarkable, considering the mess around here. But he is unconscious. No telling what's going on inside that head."

They stabilized Andy on a gurney and placed him in the ambulance for transport to Pitt Memorial Hospital. The drivers of the truck and car which collided with the trailer suffered minor injuries and were taken to the hospital in a second ambulance.

Emily Waits

Emily arrived at the tennis courts at 6:30 and sat down on a bench to tie her shoes. She waited joyfully. Just the thought of seeing Andy made her happy. Any moment her world would make his appearance. She imagined their embrace and smiled.

By 6:45 she began to look more often at the entrance, hoping to see Andy. She knew the trip from Jacksonville took one hour and twenty minutes. If Andy had left work at 5:00, he should be here by now. Maybe he had to work late.

By 7:00 she was anxious. She began to pace back and forth. She stared at the entrance and looked as far down the street as she could see. She strained to see Andy coming. She did not want to believe he may have suffered some misfortune. She tried to force herself to believe that he may have had to work late or something like that.

At 7:30, Mary, an acquaintance of Emily, came to the courts with a friend to play.

Emily watched and waited. She worried.

Mary and her friend played forty-five minutes. When they had finished, Mary stopped by to say hello to Emily.

"Is everything okay?" Mary asked.

"Oh, yes. I'm waiting for a friend. He's a little late." Emily had to hide her fears.

"Well, it's a nice evening to play," Mary said. She detected the fear in Emily's voice, but assumed Emily would ask for help if she needed any. She and her friend left.

Emily was alone again. It was now 8:l5. The lights on the tennis courts were controlled by an automatic timer and came on. Emily was thankful. The sun had set, and the dark had added to her fears.

By 9:00 she had to concede that something was wrong. But what? She knew that if Andy were able, he would call and ask her mother to notify her. The thought that he was not able to make a call was almost unbearable.

By 9:30 she began to consider her options. She could begin to look for Andy. But she was afraid of what she might discover. Andy would come. If he could not, she did not want to know the awful truth. She would wait.

At l0:l5 the lights were automatically cut off. Emily sat in the dark. She could not help but think that the light had gone from her life.

She considered the possibility that Andy might be dead. She was terrified.

She whispered, "Andy, where are you?"

She cried, "Please be safe."

She still hoped.

She would wait.

MY ONLY LOVE

You smiled for me...
Storming my fortress.

You called my name...
Eluding all my defenses.

You held my hand...
Entering my sanctuary.

You kissed me on the cheek...
Touching my soul.

You loved me with all your heart...
Coloring my world a crystal hue.

And if fate be so cruel,
As to leave me alone,

I'll refuse its offer of second best,
And see how long your memory lasts.

Andy's plight continued at the hospital. He lay on a bed in the emergency room. His wound had been cleansed and wrapped. He had been examined from head to toe. X-rays of his head revealed no fractures. His condition was stable, but he had been unconscious for almost three hours.

Andy began to awaken. He could hear the voices around him but could not determine what they were saying. He tried to open his eyes, but with little success. He tried to wiggle his hands and feet. They felt as heavy as lead. He was finally able to raise his right hand to his eyes and rub them. He was then able to slowly open his eyes. A nurse noticed his movement and placed his hands back by his sides.

"Try to remain still, Mr. Goodday," she said.

"Who are you?" Andy asked.

"I'm a nurse."

"A nurse?" Andy responded. "Where am I?"

"You're in Pitt Memorial Hospital."

Andy began to collect his thoughts.

"Why am I in the hospital?"

"You were in an automobile accident."

Andy continued to descramble his shattered world. He remembered his work day.

"It's Friday, isn't it?"

"Yes," the nurse answered.

He remembered his tennis date with Emily and was about to ask the nurse if Emily was with him in the accident. No, he thought, she was not. He had not arrived in Greenville. His battered brain began to properly function, but he could not remember the accident.

"What time is it?" he asked.

"Nine-forty-five."

"What time was the accident?"

"Just after six."

Andy tried to sit, but the nurse insisted he remain still.

"I need to sit up," Andy said, as he continued to try.

The nurse allowed him to sit but called for a doctor. When the doctor arrived, Andy had gained his balance on the side of the bed.

"Well, Mr. Goodday, you've had a bad evening."

"The evening's not over yet, Doctor. I need to make some phone calls."

"I'd say you're hardly able to sit. We can call anyone you want to notify."

"I have to make the call, doctor."

Andy was too persistent to be denied. The nurse, with the doctor's acquiescence, helped Andy to the nearest phone at the nurse's station. Andy called Emily's apartment. He received no answer. He call Mrs. Wheeler. She had not seen Emily. Andy assured her that everything would be all right. He sat down to think through the matter and further clear his clouded brain.

His concern for Emily energized him. He was now on a mission and that helped him gain control of his faculties. He decided that if she was not at her apartment and had not called Mrs. Wheeler, she had to be at the tennis courts. It had been almost four hours since their appointed time. Had she been waiting that long? Probably. She is one tough girl, Andy thought.

He obtained a telephone number for a taxi service from the directory and asked that a taxi be sent to the hospital emergency entrance.

"Wait a minute," the doctor said. "You're not able to go any place. Let me say again that we can notify anyone for you."

"Doctor, if this girl is where I think she is and she has been there all this time, I want to be the first one she sees."

"Mr. Goodday, you have had a tremendous blow to your head. You have been unconscious for over three hours. That's a long time. There could be internal bleeding which we have not detected. You could die."

The doctor's words were sobering. Andy thought about them. He went through a mental check list of his condition. He had good control over his movements. His eyesight was normal. He could see signs clearly across the room. He now had no trouble standing or walking. He believed he was able to take a taxi to see Emily.

"Doctor, some things are more important than life."

The doctor noted his determination. He also was of the opinion that Andy appeared to be in relatively good condition although he didn't tell Andy.

"Get him his clothes, Nurse. Get a release form too. And let him sign it."

He turned to Andy.

"Mr. Goodday, you're doing this against my advice. The release form will protect me and the hospital if something happens to you. When you have contacted the girl, come on back and spend the night with us just so we can keep an eye on you. And take it easy. Don't get too excited."

After his admonitions, he remembered Andy's telephone call and said, "Her name's Emily, is it?"

"Yes."

"She must be something."

"The best, Doctor. The best."

Andy dressed and waited for the taxi.

"I will come back," Andy called to the doctor as he went outside to meet the taxi.

The doctor could only shake his head.

PATIENCE REWARDED

Emily's longest night continued at the tennis courts. She sat on the bench alone. She had to rub her eyes dry to focus on the vehicle approaching the courts. When she saw that it was not Andy's car, her momentary excitement subsided. She then noticed that it was a taxi. She was guardedly hopeful as she watched a figure exit the taxi and pay the fare. Maybe Andy had car trouble and was just now able to come, she thought.

Her heart was pounding.

The taxi drove away leaving the figure standing by Emily's car which was parked under a street light.

The bench where Emily was sitting was in the shadows 75 yards away. She arose and walked slowly toward the figure. At 50 yards she could see that it was Andy. She felt weak from relief.

She began running and stopped just in front of Andy. She took a long, hard look just to convince herself he had really come. She then folded her arms around him and kissed his face all over.

Andy placed his arms around Emily, holding her tightly.

She kissed his bandage softly and laid her head on his chest.

"Emily, I ...," Andy tried to begin.

Emily placed her hand over his mouth while keeping her head on his chest and her other arm around him.

"Shoooo.... I just want to hold you for a while."

They stood holding each other until Emily's fears had disappeared in a flood of relief. Tears of joy flowed freely down Emily's cheeks.

Andy kissed the top of her head.

"My darling, my darling," he whispered.

He allowed Emily to hold him until she was satisfied.

"Let's go sit on the bench," Emily finally said while drying her eyes.

They walked to the bench with Emily's head on Andy's shoulder, her left hand in both of his hands, and her right arm around his waist. She wanted to be as close to Andy as possible.

"How long were you going to wait?"

"Oh, I don't know. A life time. I didn't want to go back if you were not going to be there."

"You know I came as soon as I could."

"I know that, Andy. I knew you would," she said with complete confidence.

"And I knew you would be waiting. Are we each other's stake or what?"

"We are," Emily said emphatically while she cuddled closer to Andy.

He pulled her closer.

Their world was returning to normal.

"Know this, Emily. Circumstances certainly wax and wane. Many things I cannot control. But if it's in my power, I will be here for you."

"And I for you. Andy, you are my only love."

They sealed it with a kiss.

"Now tell me. What happened to you?"

"They told me I was in an accident. I don't even remember it. I have to go back to the hospital for the night."

"Well, let's go now," Emily said with concern evident in her voice.

"No, I want to stay here with you for a while. You are my camomile. You're all I need."

They sealed it with another kiss.

And they talked on into the night as only lovers can. It was the kind of conversation one would have with an honest mirror.

THE WALK

Andy's injury healed without incident. A little three-inch scar remained. It was just enough for Emily to kiss and be thankful that it was not more serious. The accident only served to bind them ever tighter. They could think aloud to one another. They could wonder together without speaking. Their conversations became more poignant and progressively revealing. No preliminaries, no repeats were necessary. Some were expeditions. Some were light-hearted. Each established itself. Andy would lead today, Emily tomorrow. If one was down, the other would lift. Each knew the other. They were becoming one.

They revisited the state park in Goldsboro. As they approached the bench where they first sat, Andy bowed and waved his imaginary hat once more. Emily laid her hand on his, and they entered the 'carriage', started the 'horses', 'rode' to the bench and sat down.

"I didn't know it then, but you were my knight in shining armor."

"I didn't know it then, but you were the fairest of all the young maidens."

They sat together.

"What if we should discover flaws, Andy? It has all been so perfect. I'm afraid I'll wake up one day only to find I have been dreaming."

"Not likely. But possible."

He smiled.

"If we do, we'll beat and bang on the armor, together, and remove warts, together, until everything is made perfect."

Emily was comforted. She had been down. Andy was up.

"You know, Andrew Goodday, that you are also my best friend."

"I know that, Emily Wheeler."

They sat together. Emily had one arm under Andy's with her other arm tucked tightly on top.

Along The Ocean

"This week it's the beach," Andy said on one of his phone calls. "Let's take off from work Thursday so we'll have all of that ocean to ourselves."

"I'll be ready," Emily responded.

"We may not come back."

"That will be okay too."

"You pick me up. We'll be closer to the ocean from Jacksonville."

"I'll be there at nine."

The ocean was calm with the waves only two feet high. The only thing prohibiting one from seeing forever was the limited focus of the eye. The horizon was visible. There was not one cloud in the deep blue sky. Three shrimp boats trolled offshore. Emily and Andy were alone on the beach. It was autumn. The light breeze was a little cool. The morning sun was beginning to warm the air. They strolled in the ankle-deep portion of the breaking waves.

"Somebody knew we were coming, Andy. They painted the sky our favorite color."

"Do you suppose they did it for us?"

"No doubt. We're all alone here."

"All alone, are we? Be careful. The beach brings out the worst in me."

"I'm not worried. I can take care of myself."

She kicked water on Andy and ran down the beach.

Andy gave chase and splashed her.

A playful hug followed.

They collected sea shells. Some they threw back into the water. Seagulls would follow a thrown shell, hoping for an edible morsel. Sandpipers ran just ahead of the breaking waves and then followed their retreat, searching for a meal. Sand crabs appeared and then retreated into their holes.

"Is it easier to breathe here, or am I just hallucinating?" Andy asked.

"It's easier," Emily agreed.

She turned her face to the breeze. She closed her eyes and allowed her other senses to feed her thoughts.

They both took some long, deep breaths and exhaled slowly. They were quiet. They absorbed the day.

"Emily, I can see *TimeNot*."

Emily opened her eyes only to see that Andy had closed his. She closed hers to rejoin him.

"Tell me more, Andy."

"It is a place I have been looking for all of my life. If I ever stop looking for *TimeNot*, I'm afraid that not only will I certainly not find it, but that mediocrity, or worse, will find me."

"Go on."

"I see a friendly cloud directly over *TimeNot*. It rains its gentle showers and moves on only to return at regular intervals."

Andy closed his hand around Emily's, and they walked farther along the beach.

"*TimeNot* is this way."

Andy looked straight ahead indicating no direction, but he continued to walk.

Emily grasped Andy's hand more securely.

"I will go with you."

Adopting Andy's pace, she waited.

"Where do you think we are going?"

"Well, our search will almost certainly take us to our jobs tomorrow."

"That's good." She waited again. "If the gate is locked, we can at least rent a place to stay."

They smiled.

"The gate will not be locked, Emily, unless we lock it."

They walked farther down the beach.

Andy began to speak in tones hardly audible. Emily responded to his conversation in a like manner.

And they walked farther down the beach.

They knew not where their search for *TimeNot* would lead. But to an observer fixed in space, they became progressively smaller, disappearing into the distance. To an observer fixed in time, their conversation became unintelligible. To the skeptic, the presumptuous, they became fools. To those fixed in thought, the hard of heart, they became strangers.

They knew not where their search for *TimeNot* would lead. But the next step always becomes evident to the earnest traveler.

THE CORONATION

Bring forth the battered diadem,
Forged without a seam;
The coronation is begun,
For the frog who would be king.

Forever's mystery debunked,
In an eternal reign;
A thousand years one day,
All yesterdays the same.

Decay collects no treasures,
Time's ally in change,
It's bruised its last flower,
No fallen petal gained.

Beasts forever silenced,
And seas serenely calm,
Desire laid to rest,
A sailor has come home.

Tattered by the tempest,
And carved to fit the mold,
To exchange the incomprehensible,
For quiet that hugs the soul.

More softly waved the jester,
Your whispers are too loud,
Though delivered in a hush,
Sound as thunder's crash.

A remnant of my trip,
A stain not yet removed,
Shed in but a moment,
As I yield this throne to LOVE.